T0072261

VOICES OF THE LOST AND FOUND

MADE IN MICHIGAN WRITERS SERIES

General Editors
Michael Delp, Interlochen Center for the Arts
M. L. Liebler, Wayne State University

Advisory Editors
Melba Joyce Boyd
Wayne State University

Stuart Dybek
Western Michigan University

Kathleen Glynn

Jerry Herron
Wayne State University

Laura Kasischke
University of Michigan

Frank Rashid
Marygrove College

Doug Stanton
Author of *In Harm's Way*

*A complete listing of the books in this series
can be found online at wsupress.wayne.edu*

VOICES OF THE LOST AND FOUND

stories by DORENE O'BRIEN

Wayne State University Press   Detroit

Library of Congress Cataloging-in-Publication Data

O'Brien, Dorene.
Voices of the lost and found / Dorene O'Brien.
p. cm. — (Made in Michigan writers series)
ISBN-13: 978-0-8143-3346-4 (pbk. : alk. paper)
ISBN-10: 0-8143-3346-X (pbk. : alk. paper)
I. Title.
PS3615.B744V65 2007
813'.6—dc22
2006035886

This book is supported by the Michigan Council for Arts and Cultural Affairs.

∞ The paper used in this publication meets the minimum requirements
of the American National Standard for Information Sciences—Permanence
of Paper for Printed Library Materials, ANSI Z39.48–1984.

Designed and typeset by Maya Rhodes
Composed in Adobe Garamond and Univers Light Ultra Condensed

CONTENTS

ACKNOWLEDGMENTS

With deepest gratitude for their faith in me, I thank the National Endowment for the Arts, Wayne State University Press, M. L. Liebler, and Christopher T. Leland. Thanks also to my students for being such good teachers. For their boundless generosity, profound talent, and long-term friendship, I would especially like to thank Patricia Abbott, Ksenia Rychtycka, and David MacGregor. For their love, support, and stoic endurance, I thank my husband, Pat, and our daughter, Hadley.

I gratefully acknowledge the editors of the following publications in which some of these stories first appeared: *New Millennium Writings* and *Authors in the Park,* "Ovenbirds"; *Chicago Tribune* and *Clackamas Literary Review,* "Riding the Hubcap"; *Connecticut Review,* "Crisis Line"; *Cardinalis: A Journal of Ideas,* "No Need to Ask"; *Carve Magazine,* "Way Past Taggin'" and "Healing Waters"; *Bridport Prize Anthology,* "#12 Dagwood on Rye."

"Ovenbirds" was inspired by the work of Joyce Carol Oates.

"The Stalwart Support of the Obsessed" calls upon several lines from Plato's *Parmenides.*

OVENBIRDS

Maybe I'm brushing my daughter's hair and I see it on her neck, curved, white, like a small smile under her skin. Maybe I'm washing dishes and I see a blue Lincoln framed in the window, the geraniums on the sill perched momentarily on the car's hood as it glides innocently up the block. Maybe my husband touches my thigh absently, and I feel his fingers drawing heat from the pinched, discolored flesh.

My abductor took me from the mall. I wasn't supposed to be there, but I was. Brenda needed help choosing a prom dress, and Brenda's demands took precedence over my mother's. Brenda was popular. She couldn't drive me home because she was meeting her boyfriend at Louie's and didn't want to be late. Maybe if she hadn't left her credit card at Saks, or if we didn't stop at Farrell's, or if I were going to prom and had to try on dresses too. What I'm getting at is this: Timing is everything. That was his mantra.

That was the first thing he said to me when I came to in a cabin somewhere in the Catskills. I was lying on a cot with my ankles bound by what I later learned was an electrical cord. My mouth felt wet and raw, and when I moved my jaw I heard a popping sound that could have been an explosion a thousand miles away. I touched my mouth first—my hands were not bound, but they were bloody—and my lips were swollen, like balloons. When I gasped, I swallowed hard bits like Chiclets, like eggshells, like pebbles, before knowing that they were my broken teeth.

"Timing is everything," he said to me then. "I'm a very lucky man."

You may think that I'm also very lucky to have lived to tell this story, and on most days I'd say you're right. But I'm lucky for lots of other reasons, not the least of which was giving birth a decade later to a healthy baby girl, one who may grow to hate me more than I hate the man who abducted me, because I won't let her walk to school or ride the bus or go to the mall alone. Maybe you think this is impossible, my daughter hating me more than I hate my abductor. But it's not. Why? Because he could have been worse. When I came to, tasting blood and swallowing teeth and wondering why I couldn't feel my feet, I wasn't staring at a two-hundred-pound man in a black mask waving a sickle or a group of drunken bikers with chains and grudges. I consider that when I'm pushing my daughter on a swing or when I'm kneading the knots out of my husband's back after he's threaded his way through a house thick with flames. What if my abductor had sent pieces of my body to my parents over the course of a week, a month, a year? Sometimes, late at night, I try to tally up the parts of the body, to figure out how many days my captor could have kept occupied with slicing, wrapping, and mailing. It's comforting that I don't think like a lunatic, that I don't know if he'd count the lips as one or two items, the eyelids, the nostrils. What if he had been a desperate man who'd just lost his wife and, in his incomprehensible loneliness, held me forever?

But my abductor was dark haired, blue eyed, handsome, and he wore an Orioles baseball cap and jeans. He always said he was a lucky man, and he always said timing was everything, especially in the beginning. I don't know how many times I passed out that first day, or that first week, and I don't know if I really passed out or if I thought I passed out. You get disconnected somehow, unplugged, and your life becomes a collection of events that seem random, isolated, broken loose from the constraints of time and space. Waking and dreaming ran together early on, and I wondered if that was what it felt like to die. At first I wasn't scared. I wasn't anything. Maybe I was amazed that fate or God or whoever was in charge had such a dramatic conclusion in store for me, a nondescript suburban girl with a high IQ, a bad attitude (which today strikes me as pretty standard for a sixteen-year-old), and parents who loved her more than she deserved. I suppose that's an easy thing to believe, knowing now what I didn't know back when my abductor burned the skin on my thighs with his Zippo or yanked out my infected teeth with pliers: that my parents posted photos all over the neighborhood, harassed the Kingston County Police Department until four detectives were put on the case, cried openly on national television. When I watch the tape today, my mother looks haggard and desperate, resigned and broken. When I watch the tape today, my mother looks like me.

My abductor spoon-fed me tomato soup. He stroked my matted hair and hummed an unrecognizable tune into my ear, and this frightened me more than when he burned my legs. I thought of my parents then, and I thought of them for the first time as Jean and Eddie. And I wondered if *this* was how death began, with the dissolution of formal ties so that parents became, simply, people with their own lives, lives that would go on without yours.

Sometimes at night, when my husband is at work, I sit beside my daughter's bedroom door with a carving knife, praying an intruder will finally come to end my long, insufferable wait. I understand that any altercation with someone who means to do harm will be long, bloody, strenuous. That is the way my abductor has changed me: I have violent thoughts. Not about him but about strangers who stare too long at my daughter in grocery stores or call late at night when my husband isn't home. Violence has consumed me, and I weave it into my thoughts as absently as one might yawn. When I am finished with the man who has pulled my daughter from her carousel horse, he is sometimes decapitated, and even the clear vision of my kicking his head into the gutter doesn't pull me from my reverie. Sometimes, after a man has dragged my daughter into a car, I chase it down the road, my sandals slapping the pavement like war drums; I catch the car, I tear off the door, I drag the man out and force my thumbs into his eyes until they are pressed to the hilt into his skull. Only the thought that my daughter, the subject and trigger of these rescues, will witness and be scarred by my attacks pulls me back to the present, to the tomato plants or the fabric softener, the gas pump, the ironing board.

The cabin was rough hewn (that's what the newspaper articles said, *rough hewn*), and that is something else I think about: how funny the words *rough hewn* sound, like a foreign language, like the name of a mythological character, like a charm. The articles also said that in the rough-hewn cabin I was burned, beaten, and *violated*, as if burning and beating weren't violations. What the articles didn't say is that I didn't always mind being *violated* because afterward my abductor untied me, fed me, treated me like I was human. I'd never had sex, although I'd lied about it to Brenda, who'd shrugged as if already quite bored by the whole business. When my abductor *violated* me, I wondered if I was being punished for lying about having sex, or for hating my parents, or for being foolish enough to approach a strange man who had called out to me in the parking lot.

Between beatings and violations and tomato soup, I blamed myself for my predicament, and that's when it became bearable. That's when I said goodbye to everyone, bequeathed my tapes to Brenda and Hap, my books to Moira, my locker to Deb. Later I took the locker back, figuring no one would want it after learning what happened to me.

So, the rough-hewn cabin, the rough-hewn cabin, the rough-hewn cabin was very small, one room, I think, with a dingy shower curtain separating the beds where we slept, my abductor uninterrupted and free, me bound and chasing dreams that melted into reality so seamlessly that I was never certain where I really was. The outhouse, about forty yards from the front porch, was dwarfed by red pines and invaded by skunk cabbage. I wasn't able to use it until my ankles healed, and so for an eternity I lay in my waste and wondered how my abductor tolerated the stench and refuse to which he contributed his ejaculations; sometimes I grew embarrassed, although now I find that hard to fathom.

My husband's back grows into a wall of flame at night, an impenetrable barrier, and only then do I feel safe enough to sleep. I often believe he is made of fire, having lived in it for years, having sucked its black smoke into his body and bent it to his will. Now he can tame fire, as he can tame my fears, and his back, a constellation of scars etched by falling embers, bursts into flame just for me. "You don't want this," I told him when we first met. "I'm not who you think." But he wanted it, wanted everything, wanted to save me the way he'd saved snarling dogs and trembling women and shrieking children tossed from upstairs windows. "Tell me," he said, "let me help you carry it," and I started, "The rough-hewn cabin, the rough-hewn cabin, the rough-hewn cabin . . ."

"Timing is everything," my abductor said the day the sun slashed through the window over my cot and the birds sang just like I remembered them singing in my former life. Then he snapped the shower curtain across the rusted pole, something he'd never done before nightfall, and the tears came before I even knew, the tears came because he was doing something different, something that made the tears come without a reason. The thump was loud and hard, and the boxsprings whined, and the force of it sent his bed skidding across the floor. The newspaper articles said she was a bartender in her forties, last seen at Micky's Tavern. What the articles didn't say was that she must have known more about life than I did, because she screamed and thrashed and called him names I'd never heard a woman say before, and my abductor did the only thing he could think of to shut her up: he tore open the curtain. "Omigod," said the woman, and she saw her future then, and she clawed at him with her bloody hands and later, when she was in the trunk of the Lincoln, he smiled at me when he said that I would go along the next time, too. There were no landscape features I could memorize, no gnarled trees or scorched fields, no waterfalls or logging roads as we circled farther up the mountain to bury the woman who had called my abductor a *pin dick,* a *cocksucker,* a *child fucker.*

"Do you hear that?" my abductor asked as he stared into the flame of his lighter, the early sun blinking through chinks in the wall, the cot listing where he sat on its metal edge. "It's an ovenbird." I imagined the bird wheeling overhead, splashing in the updraft, crying out simply because it could. My abductor then blew out the flame and turned to me. "It's saying *teacher,*" he laughed, and when I didn't look at him because I never looked directly at him, he put his lips to my left ear and squawked, "*Teach-*er! *Teach-*er!"

What if I told you it was all a dream, a nightmare so real I tore at the sheets and cried bitterly, my tears mounting in waves that extinguished the flame of my husband's back? Sometimes I believe that to be true, but then there are the articles. Why have I kept them? Not because I need them to remember; I have memorized them all, and I know them better than I know the real thing that happened in the rough-hewn cabin. I know that I was "only a child," that I was "seen traveling in the passenger seat of a sky-blue Lincoln Continental," that my "abductor had killed four women in his rough-hewn cabin and buried their mutilated bodies deep in the Catskills."

"Penny for your thoughts," my abductor said as he dropped into the driver's seat of the sky-blue Lincoln Continental. On his face and his hands and his clothes—I told the police, my mother says I said these words—were all that was left of the woman, and this is something he must have said to me, something I couldn't have thought up myself. He had left me alone in the car as he carried her off into the hemlocks like a caveman, and I sat there for a hundred years waiting for the man who had abducted me, the man who had pummeled my face with a paperweight, the man on whose shirt I might later be found. I waited for him like one who waits for the hurricane, the vendetta, the end of a long fall. Did I think about escaping? Not really. Why? I don't know, although I'm convinced I knew then. What was I thinking in those minutes, those hours that passed while my abductor stabbed into the club moss and uprooted bead lily, cutting a grave for his crime? Maybe I was thinking about Jean's Hummel collection, maybe I was thinking about Brenda's prom dress, or maybe I was thinking about nothing at all. When the man came back to the Lincoln after completing his dark task, after the chucked shovel ricocheted savagely off the rusted trunk walls, after Jean once again did not rush into the wilderness to decapitate my abductor, he said, "Penny for your thoughts." I shrugged because I had lost my voice, and I would experience an eternity of events before finding it.

The article said that the land abutting the cabin was "old-growth triple-canopy forest set among gray sandstone peaks," and even today I think that sounds beautiful. But it is only the sound I find lovely, because the actual beauty of the mountains and the trees feels forever lost to me. After I read my daughter to sleep with fairy-tale stories of magic mountains and happily ever after, dark forests and sleeping death, I lie awake teasing the flames from my husband's back, envisioning myself chained to a bed inside the gingerbread house until my husband thrashes through "old-growth triple-canopy forest," hacks into the candy-coated cottage, and forces my abductor into the flaming mouth of the stove. It can happen anywhere. Snow White's dwarfs, the three little pigs, Little Red Riding Hood never stood a chance against the evil weighed against them, and their survival, a triumph of innocence over strategic and cultivated darkness, could occur only in a tale.

My husband came in from the cold, he came in from the rain, he came in from the fire. He wept, and he trembled, and I understood that something had happened; I understood that he had been broken. And so I stroked his wet hair, and I hummed into his ear, and I spoon-fed him soup. I freely accepted the power that my husband's vulnerability had thrust upon me, and in that brief moment I saw through the eyes of the keeper, the captor, the tyrant: I knew then what my abductor had felt when I accepted, when I appreciated, when I *needed* him.

My husband told me the long, horrific story of the old Victorian writhing in flames, the cupola smoking, the small dresses crumpling like dead flowers. But his story ends the way every tragedy ends: *He had her, and then he lost her.*

That's the way my story ends, although my story never really ends.

One day we drove down from the mountains, leaving behind the ovenbirds and the rough-hewn cabin, although neither of us knew it then. He said he was feeling lucky; he even let me sit upright in the passenger seat. We pulled into a grocery store parking lot, and he left me alone in the car, and I waited a hundred years. Then I saw them, the candles flickering in the restaurant window next door, and I gazed at them until the sun fell into the faraway roofs and the night came on suddenly, like a shock. And then I gave up. I opened the passenger door, I stood up, and I walked. Why? Because I thought my abductor had abandoned me, because ten minutes felt like ten years, because I was mysteriously drawn to the heat of those distant flames. The article said that after twenty-nine days I "seemed to have sleepwalked out of the wilderness and into the Parthenon," where I was hidden in the kitchen until police arrived. It seemed absolutely normal to me then, walking into the kitchen with the manager, past the spitting grills and the gleaming stoves, the bubbling pots, the burners ablaze. It may seem odd to hide a visibly broken, traumatized girl behind a towering wall of heating lamps, but I couldn't speak and no one knew what my captor looked like. There are no photos of my limping into the free world with my swollen face and my pumpkin smile, my blistered thighs and my ratted hair, my twisted visions and my night sweats. But there is a photo of my abductor alongside a dark, dark story, and for the first time I understand that he is ugly.

What if my abductor had taken me ten years earlier? Ten years later? What if I had fought like the other woman? What if he hadn't left me in the car alone while he waited in line at the grocery store, scanning magazines, eyeing women, feeling lucky? I don't know what happened any more than you do. I should, but I don't. Only once have I looked through the eyes of my abductor, have I felt empowered by weakness as it trembled against my chest and told a timeless, tragic tale, so I have to imagine that my story ends like this: He exited the grocery store humming a tune I have yet to place, and his expression, one of shock and fury after seeing the empty car, turned into awe. And maybe, as my abductor peered into the grocery bag, stared in wonder at the tomato soup cans nestled at the bottom, his awe at my bravery turned, fleetingly, into love. I don't believe he struggled like they said, and he never carried a gun that I saw. But the article said that he drew a gun, and then he was dead. In other words, our story ends like this: *He had her, and then he lost her.*

For a while I didn't hate my abductor because of the scars on his thighs, his bent and broken fingers, the seeds of fist and fury that were planted in him long before he understood what would grow. Then I had my daughter, and I hated him because I didn't know if what he planted in me would blossom into a dark, never-ending inheritance. And I hated him because I lost the person I could never know and never be, perhaps a woman with an easy openness and a carefree spirit, a mother who could teach her child to trust in herself, in humanity, in God. But then there's this: What if I had never been abducted and turned out worse? Sick, or drug addicted, or suicidal. Maybe my abductor rescued me from a fate worse than abduction. Maybe this is rationalization. But I'll never know, and this is something else my abductor has taken from me.

There was a letter, and at first its words came to me as from a fog, from a place that slipped away when I tried to close my fist around it. So I opened my hand, and I read the letter, and it said, "I forgive you." It was tucked into Revelations in a Bible found in the rough-hewn cabin, and I thought my abductor was forgiving me for being who I was, for being a montage of attributes that generated in him the undeniable need to hurt me. But the letter was addressed to a woman made of fury and fire, one with an undeniable need of her own, one with an inventive repertoire of punishments for her only son. And there was a map, and on it the words "they are all sleeping in the mountains," and above those words five sites were marked in red: four of them held the mutilated bodies of his other victims, and the fifth, "located on the eastern slope of Bearpen Mountain where it overlooks the Schoharie Creek Valley," was the place he had chosen for me.

It's always this dream, on the quiet nights when sleep comes like an old friend and memories don't claw and scratch at my shuttered mind. The mountain cracks open, and four ovenbirds ascend from its craggy depths, and I watch them weave seamless patterns across the clean white sky. And in my dream I try to rise with them, to splash madly in the updraft, to cry out simply because I can, but I remain earthbound, voiceless, envious. In the morning the dream accosts me quietly, as if through a shroud or a fog, through the same murky curtain that veiled my eyes for twenty-nine days. Only later, when I hear the sparrows calling overhead, or when I see newsreel of a volcano spitting its fiery glory skyward, or when I read about blackbirds baked in a pie, does the dream step suddenly from the shadows.

There is a scar—curved, white, like a small smile under my skin—on my neck where my abductor burned me with a bottle cap. Maybe he held the ridged edge of the cap in his twisted fingers while heating the opposite side with his lighter, or maybe I flinched, or maybe he was killed before he could complete the circle. My daughter has the same smile on her neck, although my husband insists he can't see it, but it is there, just below her right ear, a survivor's smile, a sympathy smile, an inheritance.

What can I do but be vigilant? Lightning doesn't strike twice, but even if it did, could I stop it? Is there any use in believing that we all sign on for something in this life, that we freely choose to enter a story we know will end in tragedy? I don't go to church; I don't beg God to watch over my daughter; I don't pray for the redemption of my abductor's soul. I believe in the small things, the things I can live in one moment or hold in the small of my hand: the thin strand of hair over my daughter's right ear, the stippled geranium pot on the kitchen window ledge, the strength of my husband's callused hand as it hovers, gently, over my thigh.

RIDING THE HUBCAP

Through the window I watch Michigan corn bleed into Ohio wheat, and pungent tobacco become flat miles of soy before we hit the rice fields of Mississippi. By the time we reach Biloxi I think Mason will drive until our threadbare tires are buried deep in the mud at the bottom of the Gulf. By then I don't care, and Mason cares even less.

"You smell rank," I say.

Mason laughs. "Bang, bang," he says as he points his .38 at my left ear. "You're dead, little man."

We grew up in Bad Axe. In kindergarten Mason cracked every crayon in my sixteen-pack box, in middle school he broke my thumb with a ball-peen hammer at his dad's tool-and-die shop, and in high school he hacked into my locker and stole every one of my Hendrix tapes. So why am I slumped in the cracked vinyl passenger seat of his rusted Delta 88, four states from home and hurtling toward the end of the line? That's a question I've asked myself countless times, although by now the answer doesn't really matter.

Mason got me a gun too, but I don't carry it in my pocket. I leave it on the floor in front of me, buried under the newspapers we buy every day. The seams on Mason's left pocket tore from the weight of his gun, so he shifted it to his right, where it pulls his jacket out of shape as it strains for the level surface of the seat. I liked it better when he kept it on the left side, but I also like that I can see it at all times now. We haven't eaten since stopping at a Taco Bell drive-thru in Laurel late yesterday, and my body wants food even though the thought of eating makes me sick, makes me think about all the things we've done and all the things we shouldn't have done. The husks in my teeth from the stale popcorn we ate in Memphis remind me of the Michigan cornfields, back when we were still just young and stupid. The flattened buns on the fast-food burgers take me back to Ohio's wheat fields, and I now imagine those tall, fuzzy stalks were waving at me alone, were planted there five generations ago for no other reason than to tell me to turn back. The Marlboros I've been smoking to take off the edge make me long for the tobacco fields in Kentucky, for the time right before it was too late.

After high school some of the kids left town to go to college—Central, Michigan State, Northern—but Mason and I looked forward to a big bunch of nothing. After the herds thinned, I'd look up from my caramel sundae or my comic book and Mason would be there. Then one day he asked if I wanted a job at his dad's shop, and I felt like I'd finally been rewarded for years of patience and passivity. Jobs, or at least good-paying ones, were hard to come by, but when the wrestlers and the football players his dad preferred to hire rushed headlong into their dreams, leaving Bad Axe behind like a bad memory, I fell into it.

"You'll start at eight bucks an hour," Mason said. "That's a dollar less than everyone else got."

"Okay," I said, refusing to get mad just because he wanted me to.

The next morning when I reported to work, his dad said he had three rules: don't be late, don't wear earrings, and don't hurt yourself on the clock.

"If you're late, you're fired," he said. "If you wear earrings you're a fag, and if you get hurt on the job I'll kick your ass. I swear to God I will, even if I have to wait till you're out of the hospital to do it."

Mason and his dad laughed, and I laughed too, although I knew they were at least half serious and that they didn't really care if I laughed or not. After a couple months of punching holes in steel with an industrial press and not complaining about the cuts on my hands that never healed, Mason started hanging out with me at lunch.

"I fucked Mary Matoya," he said as I sat on a bench behind the shop one day, struggling my sandwich out of its flip-top baggy.

I knew this was impossible—Mary Matoya was smart, nice, and pretty, a local rarity so far beyond any of our wildest hopes that I didn't even comment.

"You don't believe me," he said. "But I did."

"Then how come you never hung out together? Why didn't you take her to the prom?"

His laugh was dark, and I knew I was in over my head, that he was light-years ahead of me in bullshitting and that I was being set up, again.

"Fucking doesn't have to be *consensual*," he said, stretching out the word as if he'd just learned it and wanted to get it right, and I put down my sandwich.

"You're a damn liar," I said, and he shrugged. That's when I knew he was telling the truth. I wondered why Mary hadn't told anyone, why he didn't get in trouble. But that was long before I understood how the world really works, how if you're crazy enough, you can do anything.

"Here." Mason shoves two quarters at me as he pulls up to the newspaper box. I jump out and he circles the block, and for a second I imagine he just keeps driving. But he doesn't, and I get back into the car and search the paper for us.

"So, we still superstars?" he asks cheerfully.

"Shut up," I say. "Just shut up."

"You need some food," he says. "You're getting cranky."

I imagine a thick porterhouse smothered in onions, and then I vomit all over the paper. Mason just laughs and laughs.

Two weeks after I started working at Delta Tool & Die, Mason called me over to the tool bench where six years earlier he'd slammed a hammer into my thumb, and he showed me his stash of porn magazines. The women in them were beautiful in a slutty sort of way, and while I would have gladly dated any one of them,

I understood that these were not girls I'd take home to meet my mom, who wore gold crosses around her neck and lived only for the day she could meet her maker and be reunited with my father, who I imagine is asking God to take his time about it. My dad would have liked these women, and I think he would have understood why I liked them too. If he were here, I would have talked to him about Mary Matoya, about the women in the magazines, about the type of desperation I don't think I'll ever understand. But he's not, and understanding desperation isn't going to help me now.

The newspaper photo follows us from Kentucky to Tennessee, and until this afternoon I think we may have lost it somewhere in Mississippi. But it's there, under the fold, covered with last night's dinner.

"What now?" I ask, and Mason says, "Louisiana."

"How 'bout Mexico?" I say, and he says, "Why not?"

When I look at the map spread across my knees, the impact of what amateur fugitives we are hits me, and I'm suddenly discouraged by the sad state of law enforcement in America. The life had gone out of us two states ago, and we aren't so much running as limping along, almost hoping to get caught. At least I am. Maybe no one saw the car, but the cops have a clear picture of Mason in his black sunglasses looking like a terrorist, me standing dazed before the Hostess snack display. Where are they?

Six months after I started working at the shop, when my palms were etched with white scars from metal shards and my biceps had grown to the size of cantaloupes, Mason pulled up to the bay doors in his rusted Delta 88, late for the third time that week. I didn't see what happened, didn't even see his dad walk right past me and into the first act of the drama we are now living, but it ended with Mason needing eighteen stitches and a lower arm cast. He recruited me then, I can see that now, because he hated his father and hated that he was just like his father. Maybe he was hoping that I, with my do-gooder mother and my church every Sunday and my *please* and *thank you,* could save him from himself. But Mason's past was cut in him deep, deeper than the church or my mother ever cut into me, and his darkness swept over us and carried us far beyond any place my mother or the church could have warned me about.

"Ever been to the Gulf?" he asked the day his cast came off.

"No," I said. I'd actually never been more than twenty miles outside Bad Axe, but I didn't say that.

He flicked his cigarette into the field behind the shop. He was James Dean and Jim Morrison and even Hendrix, all the guys I admired and feared, all the guys I was both depressed and re-lieved I wasn't like. At that moment I hated his old man, maybe hated him even more than Mason did, because I knew that Ma-son wasn't running to the Gulf as much as he was running away from his dad. I hated his old man because I didn't have mine, and because he had Mason and let everything get so screwed up. So I hated him in that mixed-up way you hate someone but still talk to them, still act like things are okay because your hatred isn't going to change anything.

Mason shoved his fists into his pockets and said, "We're takin' a trip." It's easy to say now that there was something else in the way he said those words, something ominous and heavy as lead.

It was like he could see into the future, like he knew I would go with him even though I didn't know it myself. I had no intention of losing my job or leaving my anguished mother, but within twenty minutes he had me convinced that his dad would get over it and that we'd stop at a phone booth at least once a day to call Ma. He said we'd climb mountains and meet girls, swim under waterfalls and eat Creole. At first I was on the fence: I was drawn to and repulsed by Mason the way I was drawn to and repulsed by assassins. I wanted him to like me, to teach me to be tough and to respect me, but most of all I wanted to stop being scared of him. And for a while, when he slapped me on the back and said he'd pick me up at three, I did.

We slammed onto I-19 doing seventy, and the next thing we did was lose a hubcap. I can still see it spinning like a saucer over a bean field in Ubly, I can still hear myself offering to fetch it, and I can still hear Mason saying, "Fuck it." The lost hubcap and Mason's defeated tone were early signs of the things to come, but I missed them. We ate fast food every day and stayed in roadside motels with rusted swimming pools and mildewed bedspreads. We'd put five hundred miles on the car in one stretch and then camp out at a Motel 6 for two days. We threw Frisbees and baseballs in parking lots at midnight, and we made fun of the football players and the wrestlers who were still in school while we'd struck out on our own. And for the first time in my life I felt free. Free of my mother, free of his dad, free of the image of myself that I had when I lived in Bad Axe and worked at a place that tore little pieces of my flesh off each day. This may sound ridiculous, especially now, but I could have lived on the road forever.

She's talking on the phone, twisting the cord around her finger and giggling like the girls on TV. But she's different from the giggling girls on TV. She looks more like the women in the magazines, not beautiful but slutty. Mason slams a six-pack and a can of Pringles onto the counter as I top off my Slurpee, and she says, "Just a sec." Mason slides his sunglasses down his nose and smiles at me, and I know he's looking at the bra strap draped across her arm, the flesh spilling out of a blouse that looks two sizes too small. When she plunks down the receiver, Mason pushes up his shades and smiles.

"That it?" she says, and Mason just stands there. "That it?" she says again.

"And a Slurpee." I hold up the sweating cup as I make my way toward the counter.

She glances at my drink, then starts tapping buttons on the register until Mason reaches over and tucks his hand under her left breast. The girl slaps his arm off and yells, "What the fuck? Fucking pervert." She steps back and touches her breast, as if comforting it, and Mason just laughs because he doesn't see what I do. A man—who I figure is the manager—steps from between two coolers in back, and he has a gun aimed at the back of Mason's head. What I don't see is that Mason has a gun too, and it's aimed at the girl, and she stares at it like it's alive.

"Take off your shirt," Mason says, and I wonder what would have happened if the girl hadn't looked toward the back of the store, hadn't looked into the eyes of the man who was making his way steadily up the candy aisle, the gun clutched between his hands like a prayer. Mason swings around shooting, and he takes out a freezer door before catching the man in the chest. Then he turns back to the girl, who is stuffing money into a paper bag, and says, "Take off your shirt." She screams and he tells her to shut up and hit the floor. He grabs the money and heads for the door, and when he looks at me, it's almost as if he's forgotten I'm there. "Here." He throws the bag at me, and it slaps my chest and falls. "Get in the car," he yells, and I run out of the store and into the empty parking lot, the Slurpee still in my hand. I get into the car, and Mason gets in a few minutes later with the bag of money, a second gun, and the six-pack.

"This is for you, little man." He throws the gun at me, the gun I'd later wish the man had killed him with, and after I catch it, I realize my prints are all over it.

"I don't want it," I scream. "What the *fuck* are you doing?" I throw the gun on the floor at my feet.

"I'm killing them before they kill me," he says. "Simple as that."

"You could've killed *me*," I say. "What the fuck is wrong with you?"

Mason smiles and says, "What the hell do *you* have to live for?"

For a split second I think about shooting him, about picking up the gun and plunking a bullet in his skull. But instead I just sit there thinking about what he said, staring at the shiny gun on the floor, teetering over the abyss.

"We need to call an ambulance," I say as Mason tools calmly out of the parking lot, but then I figure the girl has already done that. I won't know until the next day when I read the *Lexington Star* that Mason has shot her too and that neither she nor her father, the store manager, ever makes it to the hospital. The camera

that shot us was mounted right above the fish-eye mirror behind
the counter, and the picture in the paper shows Mason staring
right into it, capturing the precise moment he saw the slutty girl's
father stalking up the aisle with his gun raised.

I think about running away, turning myself in, killing Mason. I
think about all the times I should have killed him and didn't—
when he stole my tapes, when he told me he raped Mary, when he
killed those people at the convenience store. I wait for a chance,
and even though now I can see there were plenty, I didn't see
them then. Maybe it was the way Mason trained his gun on my
skull and said *bang*, or the way his hand seemed made to hold a
weapon. Maybe it was the feeling of being trapped somewhere
between reality and dream, a place where going back to Ma's disappointment and his old man's fury was a worse sentence than
ticking off the miles with a lunatic. Maybe I believed him when
he said I had nothing to live for, although I don't recall believing
in anything back then.

I call Ma from a phone booth in Houston, and when she realizes
it's me she says, "The Lord is my shepherd, I shall not want," and
I know she's seen the papers. I figure FBI agents wearing headsets
and holsters line our sofa, place their chipped coffee cups on yel-
lowed doilies each time the phone rings, so I let her pray until
Mason becomes suspicious and clicks down the metal phone tab.
It doesn't matter because I know they'll be staked out like a picket
fence around the Mexican border, and I wonder if I should start
carrying the gun in my pocket. I'm not going to die for Mason or
die because I have nothing to live for. I'm going to die because I'm

stupid: too stupid to know that Mason had a gun, too stupid to realize he'd never planned to go back, too stupid to see that even Hendrix, screaming "Manic Depression" from my stolen cassette, had been warning me since Dayton. By the time we reach Texas, I realize I'm as good as dead and that parts of Mason were dead long before we left Bad Axe. What I can't figure out is why he took me along. Maybe he didn't want a savior as much as he wanted an audience, and I don't think he cared if it was me or Mary Matoya or even the retarded kid we called Gilly. Mason just refused to go down alone.

I keep smoking. I stop eating. I start carrying the gun in my pocket. If they're waiting for us down the road and they look like they mean business, I'll place the gun to my chest and shoot, a sort of tribute to the dead guy in the convenience store, one that probably no one will get. But if they're reasonable I'll be reasonable too. *Either way,* I think, because I'm too tired to be worried or afraid or to care anymore about how it goes down. Ma will pray for me, and I'll be with Dad, and she'll probably be jealous. Being with Dad will be all right; we can talk about all the mistakes I've made, all the missed opportunities, kind of like reviewing the plays in a football game after it's all done and the score's set. He'll point out the warning signs: the hubcap, the wheat fields, the Hendrix tape. He'll ask why I didn't vamoose when Mason stole a pound of ham and a carton of cigarettes from the Citgo in Springfield, when he skipped out on a motel bill in Newport, when he kept heading south even though we'd run out of cash.

We're in the middle of nowhere, headed west, cruising alongside the sweet sorghum fields just outside Laredo when blue lights start bouncing off the rear window. There are hundreds of them, it seems, and suddenly I think of a missed opportunity—I've never been to Vegas. Mason guns it, but his hand is already in his pocket. I stare out the window, imagine myself riding on a hubcap as it flies off into the distance, over the tall sweet sorghum shafts toward the sun. It is a nice image, and I decide to keep it for later when I'll need it. Then I pull out my gun—the dead man's gun—and slip off the safety. The police cars keep up with our junker easily, and for a minute I imagine we'll ride along like that until we either hit Mexico or run out of gas. But then, in real Wild West fashion, they start shooting at our tires. When the left rear explodes and we swerve into the field, Mason guns it until the car is surrounded by sharp brown shoots and the tires spin in the dirt. He jumps out and starts thrashing through the field like a wounded bull, and I climb out and follow him, thinking there is no way in hell these guys will be reasonable under the circumstances: no cooperation and no witnesses. Mason is kneeling on the ground laughing when I catch up to him, and he says, "I don't have any bullets." But when we hear the brittle reeds behind us snapping, Mason turns and raises his gun. I see a dark suit picking its way carefully through the stalks, so I raise my gun too. When the suit is nearly on top of us, I swing to my left and squeeze the trigger. Then I stand, arms raised, but instead of riding the hubcap into the sun like I planned, I watch the blood seep slowly out of Mason's skull, smell the sticky-sweet syrup of sorghum in my hair, hear the familiar sound of Mason's voice as he laughs and laughs and laughs.

Tonight I speak with a girl whose hair is on fire, a drunk weaving down the interstate in his Rolls, a woman who fails her fifth attempt at suicide by choosing too thin a rope. My voice, as always, is calm and firm: "Drop the phone and put your head under a faucet," "Check for traffic, pull to the shoulder, and tell me where you are," "Don't you know how much your family loves you? How much I love you?" I reserve that final statement for women trying to kill themselves. Call it desperate flirtation.

I answer phones at a volunteer crisis center, which means that two nights a week I pit my practiced advice and little white lies against murder, mutilation, and suicide, and I usually win because people who call don't really want to hurt anybody, even if they think they do. I lie because the truth is ugly, and the truth is this: life is hard, and it only gets harder, and many of my callers are in situations so desperate that even their gods can't save them. But I can. I say, "Get out of the house," "Drink milk mixed with mustard," "Unlock the door for the paramedics." I tell them to speak

slowly, to lie down, to stay on the line. What I don't tell them is
that they are talking to someone who is at least as screwed up as
they are. After all, what type of person offers to talk people off
ledges for free? Holy Rollers, Busybodies, and People Back from
the Brink. I belong to the latter group, but I never say this to those
who call, that I returned from the dead twice before shelving my
knives and my pills, because they would know then what sorry
shit they were in if I was their bottom-line savior. So I say, "Don't
give up" and "I love you," when sometimes I'd rather just sit and
marvel at the human predicament as it buzzes in graphic detail
through the phone lines.

I am a stockbroker, and the fact that I haven't swallowed some
Clorox after this long-term market plunge says a lot about how
I now view life: I can survive anything. We all can, though some
of us won't believe it and as a result act in strange and remark-
able ways. The world is a large-scale theater of the absurd, and I
get small glimpses of it every Monday and Wednesday evening
from eight to midnight. Don't get me wrong: I was once one of
them, hanging over the abyss, no stranger to the void, actually
craving the void, but one thought brought me back. Maybe it
was Handel's *Solomon,* or the heft of a barbell, or the taste of
Fudgsicles. These are the things that run through your mind—or
through my mind, anyway—and suddenly I realized that music
and ice cream were better than nothing, could be used to wage
war against my quiet desperation. But the pull of the void was
strong, strong enough to again find me teetering on the edge, bat-
tling the darkness with small things: tree bark, baseball, popcorn.
Understanding and surviving it doesn't make me an expert, but it

makes me something, and this something makes me think that I can help them and that maybe they can help me. A give and take, a balancing of the scales, an investment that had once paid off in hope.

But lately it's more demoralizing than hopeful. Take the guy who shoots his collie and then calls to say he's turning the gun on himself. Where does he find the composure to call in after killing the dog and before killing himself? I convince him to unload the gun, but the next day I call the Humane Society anonymously in case he shows up for another dog. Sometimes instead of protecting my callers from the cold, cruel world, I try to protect the world from my cold, cruel callers.

I'm thinking about this, how I can determine if my callers are bigger threats to themselves or to others, when a woman calls from her bathtub, says she's going to slash her wrists and then yank in her FM radio. It is to my credit that I don't use the term *overkill*. Dot had been abused—mentally, emotionally, physically—by her current boyfriend, who sounds a lot like her former boyfriend. She says she wants to talk, so we do. It's okay to tie up the line—there are lots of people here with savior complexes working to save the lives of others in lieu of living one of their own.

"Have you been raped, Dot?" I ask, trotting out my litany of "abuse questions."

"I'm not sure," she says.

I think about that for a long time. Maybe the boyfriend beat her up after consensual sex, or he beat her up during rough sex but she didn't know it, or he knocked her out and raped her while she was unconscious.

"Have you filed a police report?" I ask.

"No," she says. "I ran a bath. Then I looked for the razor blades, but I didn't have any. So I got a paring knife, but that looked really small, but I already know my steak knives are dull . . ."

These are not the words of a woman bent on dying but the words of a woman bent on bending someone's ear.

"Listen, Dot," I say. "I want you to get out of the tub, put away the knives and the radio, and call the police. You should file a restraining order against your boyfriend. Anyone who makes you want to hurt yourself is dangerous to you."

"You're really nice," she says. "Nothing like Sven."

Sven, I think. *What next?*

What comes next is a series of calls from a man who says aliens are rooting through his cupboards for cheese, for spices, for oil. I want to ask if they are making pasta salad, but instead I ask if they're threatening him, if I should send the police. He asks if I think he's crazy.

"Of course not," I say. "I hear these things happen all the time."

"Huh," he says. "They're eating me out of house and home."

He won't give me his address, says the aliens have stolen his memory. How, then, does he remember what items the aliens are seeking, and how does he remember why he called in the first place? He'd have answers to these questions, sure enough, since his explanations are not bound by the parameters of logic. I finally write him off. When he says the aliens have offered to take him back to their planet, I say, "Have a safe trip."

Dot starts calling weekly after our first talk. Wednesday nights. Ten o'clock. Sven has broken her utility tub, Sven has unplugged her refrigerator, Sven has dug up her pepper garden. Sven sounds like a real asshole.

"I've had it," she hisses one night, the venom coursing through her words. "The next time Sven shows up here'll be his last."

"What about your restraining order?" I ask.

"I haven't gotten around to it," she admits. "But how's a piece of paper gonna stop him from taking a bat to my windshield? Or to me?"

"It's a start," I say. "It usually works." That's a lie, but one that often brings comfort to distraught women, a brief reprieve from fear and resignation, faith in a law enforcement system that each night we watch fail our city on the local news. But then Dot is more than a distraught woman. She is an angry, had enough, lying-in-wait distraught woman, and I actually start to worry a little bit about Sven.

"Listen, Dot," I say. "Don't do anything rash. Change the locks, file a restraining order, stay with friends for a while."

I think she giggles, a muffled little girl sound that could also be a sob. But this is Dot, whom I have come to believe might sooner cold-cock someone with a tire iron than cry over him. Maybe she attracts abusive men because she likes to fight.

"Okay," she says. "I'll file the order. But I've got a hammer under my pillow with Sven's name on it."

I don't like the sound of that, and I tell her so. I speak about blood and regret, about the permanence of bad solutions to temporary problems, about how even someone as angry as Sven can be reasoned with.

"I'm just tired," she says. "I haven't been sleeping well."

Who could sleep well with a hammer under her pillow?

"You're not thinking of taking something to sleep, are you? Like pills or anything?"

"Aw," she says. "You are *so* thoughtful."

After I hang up with Dot, the Alien Man calls back to complain about airsickness in the spaceship and the pain from the metal surveillance implant they've lodged in his skull.

"I think you should talk to someone," I say.

"I *am* talking to someone," he says accusingly.

"I mean a professional."

"You mean the FBI? Someone who specializes in abductions? Although I *did* go willingly," he adds, the logic slipping right past him and into the conversation. "But I never agreed to this implant. Bastards."

"Let's talk about that implant," I say.

Alien Man hangs up suddenly, and I imagine the Martians in his mind walking into the kitchen for some sausage or some root beer and catching him on the telephone.

You may think I'm insensitive for calling him Alien Man or for calling the compulsive masturbator Handyman or for calling the inept suicidal woman Six or Seven or, by next month, Eight. But I have to put something between their plights and my heart, something to keep them from showing up in my dreams at night, and that something turns out to be my immature intellect. Do you think that someone who's sharing his home with extraterrestrials or someone whose penis is inflamed or someone who has considered swallowing nails cares about name-calling?

Before I again speak to Dot, before I learn that Sven has placed kerosene-soaked towels around the perimeter of her house, I talk with a woman who stabbed her neighbor and with a marine whose gay lover is threatening to expose him. There is the panicked smuggler, worried the cocaine-filled balloons she swallowed will rupture, the nun who no longer knows God, the used-car salesman whose wife has fallen for the Absopure man. My tone indicates that nothing could be more natural than eating fifty grams of cocaine, than denouncing your lifelong faith, than stabbing a neighbor who's lobbed her dog's shit into your backyard, but my mind is in overdrive, negotiating ways to both gain trust and gather information from callers who are in trouble, whose victims might still be alive.

Something else happens before I again speak to Dot: the center's phones are outfitted with Caller ID. I don't know about the constitutionality of it all, but our manager seems to think that being on a first-name basis before even picking up will somehow be comforting to callers: "Hello, Anne, what would you like to talk about tonight?" she says, reading from our new script in her annoying southern twang.

"What if it's not Anne calling?" I ask.

Her retort: "What if it *is*?" It is her policy never to answer questions intelligently.

"What if it's *not*?" I repeat.

"The odds say that it is."

"What odds?" I ask, incredulous, and she says, "All of them." She's as loony as any caller I've ever had, but she holds it together with her cross and her Bible and a grant from an anonymous donor whose wife she'd rescued from the oven. She says we will take advantage of the new technology immediately, and the other gods and I nod our heads and then do what gods invariably do: whatever we want to.

On my sanest days I would find it unsettling to hear "Hello, Robert" after dialing up for a pizza or calling to register a complaint with the lawn service. I think about Alien Man and the effect this new technology could have on him; maybe he would think I was psychic, or that I was one of *them.* The girl who'd swallowed the drugs might think the phone had a tracer, that I was keeping her on the line long enough to give the police a chance to arrest her. I decide it's too risky; I won't do it.

When Dot calls the following Wednesday at ten *on the dot,* a joke I do not have the heart to tell her has long ago lost its luster, I see on my digital display that her real name is Dorothy Brautigan. It sounds pretty, classy, not the name of a woman who dates Svens and sleeps with a hammer under her pillow. She says she filed a restraining order but that he'd come poking around anyway. She didn't see him, but she smelled gas around her bedroom window and found the towels—seven of them—placed in strategic locations outside. I am relieved that she called the police instead of me, glad that they convinced her to spend the night at her mother's.

"Have they arrested him?" I ask.

"No. Said they'd question him. That's all. Said they can't *prove* anything."

"They'll question him," I say. "They'll get to the bottom of it. Maybe they'll arrest him. Or scare him off." I suddenly envision meeting Dot, impressing her with my calm strength, a bright flare against Sven's dark, dark shadow, and wonder if this occurs to me only because Sven might now be arrested, on the lam, out of the picture.

"Sven doesn't scare easily," she says. "He'll be back, and I'll be waiting."

She called the police, filed a restraining order, sleeps with a hammer, and is still being terrorized by her boyfriend. I wonder about Sven, wonder if he's really crazy enough or angry enough or hopeless enough to actually strike the match. Then I think about Dot until I can't think about her anymore, and I know when I can't come up with a nickname for her that I will simply call her Dorothy Brautigan, that I will look for that name in the local white pages, that I will sit in front of her bungalow on Monday and Wednesday nights after work, waiting for Sven and hoping he never comes.

When my own skies cleared, I was determined to do right: atone for the nasty things I'd done to my family, offset the attempted suicides, offer people the small things that I knew could save them. I wanted to balance the misery I'd inflicted with the misery I dispelled, not knowing how impossible this is. Who can weigh misery when the language of pain is not universal, can never be understood fully by anyone other than its victim? Gaining perspective while using my experience with despair and rebirth to help others, I believed, would make me whole. But I know now that we are not born to be whole; we are born to be cracked and thrown and flattened by circumstance, and our lives consist of the constant struggle to become whole, something we never were and never will be. This is what I want to say to Dot as I sit in front of her house, my palm sweaty where the phone lies across it. I want to say that the bluebells in her yard can save her, the chipped plate, the old letter; I want to say that the small things, the old things, the broken things can bring us comfort, can make us realize that we can be content without being whole. Just as I imagine ringing her doorbell, entering her house and taking her into my arms while proclaiming my small wisdom, the porch light snaps off, the front door swings open, and a small woman in a bathrobe and slippers steps out. She's wearing white gloves, and she has something in her hand—a leash, or a stick—and as she makes her way toward the street, I slump down low; maybe Sven is crouched in the bushes, on the roof, behind a car. Just as I'm about to power up the phone, just as I'm about to lower my window and call out to her, just as I'm about to create a future with Dorothy Brautigan, I notice that the strange protrusion dangling from her left hand is an aluminum baseball bat. The woman who I assume—who I know—is Dot moves with great trepidation across the front lawn, her arm stiffening, her head shifting like a wary animal until she stands, rigid, before her mailbox. It doesn't take long. As I peek at the crumpled box lying at her pink-slippered feet, I understand that Dot is practiced at breaking things.

She calls the following Wednesday, and I say, "Hello, Dorothy Brautigan." My heart races; I have all the cards; I am the cat and she is the canary.

"How do you know my name?" she asks.

"I know a lot of things," I say. "You'd be surprised."

"Well, do you know that Sven dismantled my ten-speed? That he busted up my mailbox?"

"That must be a terrible inconvenience," I say.

"The police won't do anything. Said they can't find him, but they're not really looking. Not really."

"Maybe they're looking in the wrong place."

"Well, duh," she says.

Her condescension is provoking. "Dot," I say, "the police are very busy."

"Right," she says. "Too busy to arrest a guy who's trying to kill me."

"They need proof, Dot. Real evidence."

"Well, I've got real evidence," she says. "I've got the bat he used to demolish my mailbox. He left it in the street, and I'm sure his prints are all over it."

What would you do? I figure the detective to whom she gives the bat will figure it out; even Sven can't be dumb enough to leave evidence like that. And he'll probably have alibis for the night her garden was suspiciously torn up, her bike dismantled, her yard peppered with combustible towels. For the next week I find myself thinking about Dot as I watch numbers march across the screens at work, as I bake frozen tetrazzini, as I trim the grapevine in the yard. I wonder what makes her hate her boyfriend so much that she'd set him up this way. Then it hits me: Sven doesn't exist at all.

But Dot does, and while I can't diagnose her specific mental ailment, I'm now convinced she needs help. Maybe the police will eventually figure it out, but I can save them lots of time and effort, rescue them not from a cold, cruel caller but from a sick woman in desperate need of attention. I call the precinct and tell them everything, ask them not to arrest her for the false police report, tell them I'll convince her to get help.

Wednesday comes. One pregnant teen, one shaken cop, a kid with an ice pick in his throat. "Talk to your parents," "You had no choice," "Keep still until help arrives." At nine o'clock Dot calls.

"Hello, Dorothy Brautigan," I say.

"Sven's in the garage," she says. "I can hear him."

"Maybe he's reassembling your bike."

"I called the cops ten minutes ago. Where are they? They want evidence? He's in my fucking garage."

"Listen, Dot," I say, "I'd like to give you a telephone number."

"A phone number? Shit," she says and hangs up.

Rules or no rules, I think about calling her back. If she keeps bugging the police, they'll arrest her for filing false reports, maybe even tell her I was staked out in front of her house. How would I explain that? I summon my crazy manager, who trots over in her leather cowboy boots, the fake spurs jangling.

"There's this woman who's calling for attention," I say.

"Well," she says, "why else would someone call a crisis line?"

Her condescension, not unlike Dot's, is provoking. "This woman isn't just a line abuser. She's desperate. Calling the cops, framing imaginary people, faking suicide attempts." I realize, only after vocalizing her repertoire of behaviors, that maybe Dot is more than just desperate for attention. Maybe she's certifiable. Maybe she'll hurt herself if the attention fades. "I wanna call her."

"No can do, Bucko," she says. "No can do."

So I call, and when I hear the phone being plucked from its cradle, I hang up. I'm able to confirm that she's okay without, technically, breaking the rules.

The phone rings a few minutes later, and I smile when I see

the words *Dorothy Brautigan* flash across my screen. There are worse things than befriending a lunatic, coaxing a desperate person away from the cliff with peanut butter or SnoCones, offering attention to someone for no other reason than that she needs it.

"Hello, Dorothy Brautigan again," I say, and it isn't long before I know that I've made the biggest mistake of my life.

I go to the funeral. Everyone says she looks beautiful. How would I know? All I know is that I sit in the third row on a hard wooden chair among strangers, mouthing prayers I've never heard and seeing myself doing a life sentence at the center to offset this one, to tip back the scales, to keep me on this side of the abyss. It's no comfort that the police also failed her, that they required so much evidence to arrest Sven she felt compelled to create it.

People at the center say the same things to me that I say to callers: "It's not your fault," "You couldn't have known," "He was determined." What they don't say is that he broke into her house from the garage, that his suspicions were ignited by my hang-up call, that after he hit redial and heard a strange man flirting with his girlfriend, he wrestled Dot's hammer away and swung it.

Tonight I speak with a girl who's swallowed Raid, a geek being stalked by bullies, an artist who is crafting a fine and intricate noose. My voice, as always, is calm and firm.

NO NEED TO ASK

The day before they found Trenton South's left hand in the tackle shop was what you might call a red-banner day: John and Willie was fired for smiling, Connie announced she was three months gone, and Cole got smacked in the head with a six-pound bass.

Shit rolls downhill. Everyone knows that. There wasn't a day went by I didn't wish he was dead, or worse. Here's a lesson: keep your mouth shut.

Now he's dead, and though I didn't do it and I'd bet my next two paychecks there's a list of suspects long as a country mile, I know they're headed straight for me. I look good for it, I sure do, what with me running my mouth about gutting him like a deer and stringing his carcass up behind my shed. Dammit!

Robbie, John, Willie, and Cole—they look good for it too, but me, I'm just beautiful. Robbie once backed into him with his pickup, though Robbie was drunk and they weren't at the fishery or on the clock but in the parking lot of Waylan's. Trenton South

didn't go down like the wealthiest guy or the meanest drunk or
the owner of the biggest business in town (though he was all
these things) but like a lopsided bowling pin in a sequined cowboy shirt. This, according to Robbie, who says South went down
quiet, which ain't the way he did most things. But he got up that
time.

The bastard owned the Limon fishery with its tackle shop and
its snack bar and its four bass ponds, which is where we work and
which will all go to Berniece ("spelled the opposite of nephew"
shut the hell up already, even at the funeral, for chrissakes) and
their two kids, who have red hair like straw and thick necks and
voices that make you wanna shake 'em. When I first started working the fishery, she brought 'em out to fish and I says to the boy,
a fat kid with milk-white legs and black socks, "You know how
to cast a line?" and he looks at me like his daddy always did, with
that one crossed eye and that sneer, and in a different life I could
have felt sorry for him. When he whacked me across the cheek
with his fishing pole, I almost hit him. Almost. And when his
buck-toothed sister refused to take the pole from my hand, when
she pointed her finger into my face so close I could see the tabs
of flesh where she'd chewed on it, when she said, "You stink like a
pig," I just smiled and said, "Aw, ain't she cute?"

Berniece the opposite of nephew did not scold or otherwise
restrain her children from throwing soda into the pond or casting their hooked lines at my back. I looked into that pond and
felt sorry for the bass whose spawn were so much more worthy of
life than the spawn of Trenton South, who at that very moment
were clubbing at the fish with the blunt ends of their poles. Did I
imagine digging my fingers into their fat faces and bashing their

heads against the retaining wall? There's no need to ask. Instead I took a break, made sure Cole didn't see 'em taunting the fish, and when I got back Humpty and Dumpty had tangled their lines and were kicking and slapping each other while Berniece lay sprawled across the grass. She is not a small woman, and in her floppy hat and her flowered muumuu she looked like a broken-down float.

Sure I go to the funeral; we all do. They close the fishery, and we all go only to talk about who we think killed the son-of-a-bitch. The wife? Too dumb. The kids? Too young. Robbie? Too drunk, usually. One of us, John, Willie, Cole, me. We stare at each other. Maybe.

We're huddled in a small circle at the back of the funeral parlor when Willie points at me. "You said you wanted to gut him like a deer," he says, the grin cracking the lower half of his face, and Robbie, John, and Cole stare at me. "Don't worry," Willie says, "I never heard nothin'."

I wonder if he's saying this 'cause he thinks I killed South or 'cause he wants me to lose my hearing if I find out he did.

"John ain't heard nothin' either, ain't that right?" Willie claps John on the back and John smiles. "Nope," he says. "In fact, I think it's a good idea if none of us heard nothin'."

"Maybe it wasn't one of us," says Robbie, who's been pulling from a flask ever since he entered the front door of the Faith Walks funeral home. "Guy like South probably got people lined up to kill him."

Cole's been quiet all along, his button-down shirt a noose around his neck, his head down and his boot tip moving across the floor, tracing the outline of the blood-red roses in the carpet.

"I did it," says Robbie, and we all look at him, even Cole.

Then he bursts out laughing but stops when a group of people—fat people like South and Berniece and their kids, probably kin—look at us from in front of the silk-lined, gold-etched empty casket. They're on their knees and circled around, saying goodbye to nothing, paying their respects to air. Robbie pushes the flask into his pocket.

"I ain't heard nothin', and that's it," says Willie, and everyone nods.

"But I'd sure like to," I say. "I mean, hear it and then unhear it. Know and then right after that not know."

We look at each other again, for signs, I think, for a wink, maybe an eyebrow twitch or a smirk. Nothing.

"Maybe we all did it," I say, my brain snagging onto something big, something I see looming over the horizon like salvation. "Maybe that's the story."

John and Willie smile; they get it. But Robbie and Cole just stand there looking like Robbie and Cole.

"It's like this," I say. "If they say it's one of us, we all say we did it, but we make up different stories how. And if one of us did do it, it would be smart of that person to make up a story different than the one that's the truth."

"That would confuse 'em," says Willie, "and if they can't pin it on someone sure, they'd rather just slit the net and let all the fish go."

Cole smiles; he's thinking about the fish all swimming free, maybe even seeing our faces on their bodies.

"Well, I did it," says Robbie, and I don't know if that's just Robbie being Robbie or Robbie playing like he's in court or Robbie telling the truth.

Robbie said things, but he always said things when he was drunk and he was almost always drunk. He talked about what he'd do to South if he ever caught him with Connie for real, and by that he meant off the premises of the fishery, where Connie worked at the snack bar and where South always seemed to be hungry. Robbie said things like *stab, shoot, skull, dead,* and so on and so forth. South used to stare at Robbie's woman—actually a stupid little mountain girl with big eyes and a hollow head and a knack for getting mixed up with drunks—and she'd suck it up just to get close to South's money or to get Robbie boiling, I ain't sure if it's both or which. She would wiggle and twitch around the grill like a flag in a windstorm, and South's bad eye would start spinning in its socket. I wanted to hit 'em both, but probably Robbie wanted to hit 'em more, 'specially after South made Connie cry. We didn't know why, but we found out soon enough.

Come to think of it, Robbie never acted any sorry after slamming into South with his 4x4, and lucky for him South was too drunk to know what hit him. But would any of us have been sorry? I wonder about that sometimes, like what if it was me who hit South with my truck, and what would I do if he was laying there on the ground behind my tires, out cold, that twitchy eye begging to be smeared into the pavement? My foot jerks just thinking about it, even with him already dead. That probably says a lot about me, but it says more about Trenton South. I'll get to telling you more about Trenton South, and maybe when I'm done you'll wanna run him over with your truck too, the way me and John and Willie only dream we had.

That's what we used to talk about, me and John and Willie, the crunch of the neck or the blood splattered with sequins. John and Willie are brothers, and though I ain't never outwardly agreed, I understand what folks are getting at when they say those boys share a brain. But folks don't know about the time they strung up that ol' Cajun who'd gone heavy on the feed scale or when they tricked South into believing the law consecrated his sawed-off shotgun for it being illegal. Hell, they had South almost thanking 'em when they said they told the sheriff they didn't know whose gun it was, said some customer they didn't know and wouldn't never recognize left it in the shop right before the sheriff pulled up in his squad car, carrying with him a notion to have a look around. John and Willie still got that gun and the rods and reels and who knows what else they stole right from under South's lazy eye; they more than made up for what South held back on their paychecks, as if they couldn't add up the cost of a burger and a soda at the snack bar, as if they wouldn't find out there ain't no such thing as apprentice tax. They made out all right, selling South's stuff here and there, and I'd even say that John and Willie don't seem to particularly mind that folks think they're dim, 'specially right about now. But Trenton South was a big son-of-a-bitch, and what I'm saying is this: Maybe it wasn't a one-man job. Unless that man was Cole.

Cole, he's dark. His story is what I call biblical: too long, too wide, too deep. That boy's swum in a sea of misery, and now the salt coats his gums and the kelp's snagged his feet and I imagine it ain't never letting go. Cole's got a checkerboard of scars on his back, but there's no need to ask. One thing about Cole, he loves the fish. Sometimes he talks to 'em, probably tells 'em the things he can't talk to anybody else about. So we let Cole feed the fish, mostly to keep him away from customers, who tend to treat the fish like fish. South knew how Cole felt about them fish, knew it wasn't normal, and knew he was playing with a lit fuse, but he done it anyway. He'd come in drunk, eat two burgers and a shake, make Connie wipe his big fat ugly mouth, and then tell Cole to bait his hook. Sometimes, when there wasn't any customers around—he wasn't dumb, I'll give him that—he'd reel in a fish and then swing it around until the flesh tore and the hook came loose. Sometimes he'd just take the fish off the hook and watch Cole watch it flop on the ground. Sometimes he'd carry the fish to the snack bar, slam its head on the counter, and throw it at Connie. This ain't the thing that made her cry. She was used to that.

The last time South fished he caught a beauty, a six-pound spotted bass that swung but once before the hook came loose. Then it laid on the grass, real still, and Cole just shut his eyes and damn him for letting South see him that way.

"C'mere," South yelled at Cole as he trotted off toward the fish. "C'mere," he yelled again, but Cole didn't budge. So South picks up the fish, puts the hand that would be gone presently into its mouth, and starts squawking when the fish latches on. This is a thing peculiar to the spotted bass, a small tongue covered with sharp teeth; this is a thing Trenton South shoulda known. South's red hot mad when no one goes to help him, when Cole's eyes start smiling, so he peels the fish off and then yanks it up by the tail and heads toward Cole swinging.

You'd think Cole would've killed him on the spot, would've cracked South's fishing pole, would've tried to save the fish. But Cole just turned to stone when South acted up, and it became South's business to break him.

When Berniece started bringing the kids regular, I made sure Cole didn't catch that ticket, and I told 'em that Cole was Billy the Kid's great grandson. I told 'em never to sneak up on him or to make loud noises or to say bad things to him 'cause he was genetically postponed to do terrible things. 'Course it wouldn't have taken loud noises or insults to get Cole to do terrible things to them, so John and Robbie and Willie and me always made sure he was with the locals instead of the tourists, and never with the kids. When I look back at it now, it was hard work keeping Cole away from this and that and watching Robbie watch South at the snack bar and making sure John and Willie's paws was empty when South was by the tackle shop. Being ready for anything can make you damn tired, and while I don't think I would've ever killed Trenton South, I see now I wasn't too good to do some other things to ease my load.

Take Berniece, for example. She ain't brought those kids around in a long while, not since the boy slipped face first into the pond and his sister got hit in the head by a half-full can of Co'Cola. Did I help that boy into the pond? Did I lob that shiny can at her red straw head? To that I answer, yes, ma'am, and yes, sir. I ain't no saint. Let's just say I helped them out while saving myself a whole heap of headaches.

Wanna hear the funny thing? South's body was never found. Well, not all of it. They found his hand wrapped around a Falcon Low-Rider XG casting rod in the tackle shop, the Superbowl ring he bought from some NFL washout still on his pinkie. Most of us can live without a hand, I guess, but this was Trenton South, and that was his drankin' hand. When Robbie said this at South's funeral, I thought it was some funny, but Cole just looked at Robbie like he was an unpaid bill. Then he shuffled through the door without saying nothing, not even paying his respects to Berniece, whose eyes looked like they'd been outlined in red marker. What she had to cry about I will never be sure. Maybe South was a good husband and father, but I can't see it. He was a bastard at work because he knew he was the only game in town, and he knew we weren't going nowhere. So he'd cut John's hours and give 'em to Robbie one month, and then he'd flip it around the next so everyone had a chance to hate him equal. The bad thing was he gave everyone a chance to hate each other, and that made us hate South even more. He touched Robbie's woman and made her touch him, he cheated John and Willie outta money they had to steal back, he tortured the only thing Cole could ever get himself to care for.

What did he do to me? Well, it amounts to this: while I never got out from under the nasty sneers in front of customers or the sudden price increases on burgers and soda, he never took made-up taxes outta my pay or cut my hours too much. It's like he knew things about me I didn't know myself. But don't kid yourself: He dared me to kill him in other ways and there ain't no question. Sooner or later he figured out it was my job to get the rest of the guys squared up, to keep 'em level, maybe even to keep 'em from killing him, and he had me working full time at that. It was me he was looking at when he told Cole to bait his hook; it was me he was smiling at when he ran his finger along Connie's name tag; it was me he was preaching to about how you gotta rob one guy to pay the other. Maybe I got tired of watching everyone watch South and let my guard down, or maybe South just made it too hard for me to keep him alive. Either way. Did I mention they found his foot near the edge of the biggest bass pond? How'd we know it was his? When someone stomps on you long enough, you don't forget his boots.

They dragged that pond for a month of Sundays and wouldn't let none of us in. I never saw Cole so nervous, and at first I thought they'd find something sure, but when he asked if he could feed the fish and they ignored him, I thought he was gonna break down. The stronger fish would just eat the weaker ones, and I knew he knew that, but neither of us said it. Ends up they didn't find nothing in that pond but fish and water and the rusted fender from an old Buick, so they lit out, and when they did Cole was there with a bag of pellets. He spent half a day feeding the fish, and from a distance it looked like he was throwing an invisible Frisbee over and over. But up close you saw that he was talking to the fish, his words drowned by the sound of feed sprinkling the water like rain.

The day before they found Trenton South's left hand in the tackle shop, the same hand he used to pinch Connie's tight ass, the same hand he used to slam a spotted bass into Cole's face, the same hand he used to write in the phony apprentice tax, Connie paged Trenton South to the snack bar with her big mouth. She told him something, and he told her something, and she began to bawl like a kid in front of an empty ice cream truck. Then Trenton South paged all of us to the snack bar with his big mouth. He told Robbie he wasn't gonna be tricked into paying for *his* bastard kid, that he had Connie but just that once and it sure wasn't a memorable experience so maybe it never even happened, and this got Connie bawling some more at the insult to her womanly charms or the fact that she wasn't gonna get South's money, I ain't sure if it's both or which. Robbie let loose with a slur of threats none of us could make out, which turned out to be a blessing for him after the fact. His face was pale but South's was red, and he was pointing that hand that would soon be gone at all of us.

"You think I'm blind?" he said. "You think I don't know what you're doin'?"

Since we were all doing things he wouldn't like and we wasn't sure he knew exactly what they were, we just played dumb while South worked himself into a regular tornado.

"I know what you're up to," he said, and he smiled at John and Willie and they did the damnedest thing: they smiled back. Then he fired 'em, though none of us are eager to share this piece of information with the new boss. Did he know they were stealing or did he fire 'em for being dumb enough or smart enough to smile back? Did he know it was Robbie's trailer hitch leading the charge into his flabby back? Did he know Cole spent every Wednesday afternoon mixing the pellets with raw burger he stole from the snack bar to add some snap to the fishes' diet? Did he know I kicked his son into the pond and smacked his little girl in the head with a soda pop can and that I laughed when they started yanking each other's hair out over it? That, I guess, we will surely never know.

He told us all to go home goddammit he could run the place himself, and that was the last time I saw Trenton South in one piece.

After the funeral the sheriff's waiting on my porch, and he ain't inclined to small talk.

"Where were you the night a Wednesday, August 12th?" he
says.

"Well, I'm fine, Mason. How're you?"

"I'm glad you're fine," he says. "At least one of us is fine."

This makes me laugh. Mason ain't never instigated a murder
case before, and I wanna tell him that it ain't a good idea to let on
that he's nervous, that he don't know what he's doing, but what's
the use? We all got histories cut into us so deep a little scrubbing
ain't gonna but buff the surface.

"So?" He flips open a pad a paper and pulls a pen from behind his ear, and I gotta stop myself from ordering the blue plate
special.

"I was here, just like every night," I say.

He asks if there's any witnesses and I just laugh. But he don't
ask if I said I wanted to gut South like an animal, though I imagine that story's gonna fly when he starts pointing fingers unless we
all stick to the plan.

"You going to see Cole?" I ask, nodding my head up the road
toward his place. "Yeah?" I say. "Well, you better take a deputy or
two along."

When the sheriff leaves, I drive over to Cole's with a six-pack
to watch the fireworks, but he ain't home. It's a nice night, probably 'cause South is dead (everything that is nice will be nice for
a long time because South is dead), so I drive up 245 with my
window open and I listen to the night. I think about freedom,
though I ain't sure how I can be any more free with South dead
since I plan to be at the fishery early next morning. But I won't
have to pay my way with my pride, depending on who takes over,
though I imagine whoever it is won't be real eager to make en-

emies after seeing South's body parts thrown about the premises. I go to the fishery 'cause there's nowhere else to go, and I see Cole's truck parked behind the maintenance building. Sure enough, he's out there, probably talking to the fish, and I think about sneaking up just to hear if he's confessing, not that I'd tell. But I ain't the sneaking sort, so I think I'll just offer him a beer and we'll sit together under a dark sky in a world free of Trenton South. When I get closer, I see that he's feeding the fish, but it don't sound like rainwater sprinkling the pond. It sounds like hail, like rocks, like chunks, and there's no need to ask.

WAY PAST TAGGIN'

I ain't no toy, not no more. I been writin' since I could tip a brush and a spray can, and now I can tag, piece, and get up better than Smak and Daze, and they call themselves the kings of Krylon, rulin' the buildings and billboards from midnight 'til mornin'. But I don't do what they do, fat cappin' their gang tags so everyone can see, bubble letters in gold and red across freeway overhangs and laid-up train cars. I used to do throw-ups, tag *Doom* in huge black-around-white letters on garage doors, telephone poles, the urinals at Coney Island, hell, anywhere I could reach. But that ain't art, that's just writin' your name like you learnt in kinnergarten. Listen, taggin's alright, especially for toys, but it's wack if you ain't got much else after five years.

Smak and Daze, they ain't got much else, and that's why they want me in the Bloodhounds. They say I got to get hooked up, that it ain't good writin' alone with the city puttin' cameras all up in here, that they won't bother with the face cuttin' but I gotta wear the cap with the BH on the side. I wanna ask who did that, like did their grandmas stay up late watchin' TV and sewin' these bloody letters with red thread and not askin' what it all means? What it means is Smak and Daze know I'm good, and they wanna keep me close 'cause the best writers get respect and they ain't the best writers no more with their loose taggin' and their sloppy taggin' and their ain't got no play taggin'. What I know is I'm way past taggin' and they ain't got nothin' on me. I got my own style. I got my own beefs. I got eyes in the back a my fuckin' head.

I never told no one I went to the local art school for a year as the poor, hungry black kid after my grandma showed 'em my stuff, that everything I learnt there fell right through my head, that I just stared at the old white dude who taught color and light, watched him match up colors on a wheel, watched him shade boxes and circles to make 'em jump off the page, watched him do shit I'd been doin' on the side of Bank One and Compuware for three years.

The jewelry lady was nice with her frizzy hair and her hippie clothes and her small hands she used to touch everybody like she meant it 'cause she did. She'd thread glass beads onto wires with those tiny fingers, starin' 'til her eyes were crossed, forgettin' about everything but the bead and the wire. I thought bad shit then, like I could crack her in the skull and take her purse and she wouldn't be able to figure it out 'cause her life right then was the bead and the wire, but I never did 'cause I saw that she was just like me when I was piecin': my life was the paint and the wall and the need to get them together. My life still is the paint and the wall and the need to get them together, and that's why Smak and Daze want me in their crew: I'm good 'cause I feed off the hiss of the nozzle, the rattle of the can, the masterpiece that keeps me goin' 'til I can do it all over again.

But they had no room for what I did in school, no wild style, no piecin'. I couldn't do with an airbrush what I did with the can so the teachers kept me down, kept sayin' I had to do the time. It wasn't so bad feelin' like I was in prison, but I couldn't take my art bein' in prison, the pictures and ideas stuck somewhere between my head and my hand, me feelin' full up all the time. So when I was sixteen and flyin' between funk and mind rage, I left school. I was tired of itchin' to get out while I was in, tired of the white boys tryin' to get in with or get over on me, tired of teachers tryin' to figure out what art is instead of just doin' it. Ain't no explanation for lettin' the thing inside you come out but that it gotta come out, and ain't no thing to do but love or hate the thing after it does. When I left I was full of stuff I held in for too long, things I couldn't even try to explain. Instead I just burned, got up everywhere and on anything standin' still: phone booths, garbage cans, alley walls. Didn't care right then if I got arrested or shot. I was free—no hassles, no memories. Then one night when I was piecin' Dr. Doom across the side of a dead bus on Second, somethin' come to me without me *knowin'* knowin', and it was the eyes, not X-Man eyes but human eyes, and they were so damn good and perfect I didn't care if they were on a cartoon. I thought then that maybe everything didn't fall through my head at art school, that I had memories I could let come if I was careful and didn't let 'em fuck with my head the way the ones of my mom did.

So I let in the old white dude and the hippie jewelry lady and the Chinese geek who drew faces so good it jabbed your gut to

look at 'em. They all came back in pieces—I saw the geek fleshin'
out a saggy mouth or the hippie woman twistin' a wire. They
came back when I was eatin' a Junior Whopper I begged from
the drive-thru chick or loadin' the cans into my backpack. They
came back when I jumped the fence outside the train station and
slit my leg on razor wire. They came back when I sat gaggin' in a
Dumpster while copters slashed their lights across the truck yard.
But when Ma showed up at the door of my memory, I slammed
it in her face. It's all about choices. I sleep during the day so I can
write at night, I steal or beg money to keep the paint stocked, I
remember only what'll make me a better writer 'cause writin's all I
got and all I really need.

   That's why when I'm paintin' the Black King across a buffed-
up billboard, I remember somethin' about proportion, and I work
all night and into the day, and cars slammin' down 75 honk and
the people scream, and they're happy with the proportion and so
am I. Not even Ace's gone over the Black King, and he's about
the only other writer good enough to maybe do somethin' better.
That's the rule on the street: if you can't outdo what you wanna go
over, stay the fuck off.

   Before I paint those cops shootin' rainbows from their guns
into the hearts of two gangbangers across the side of the City
County Building, I sit in the bushes for a long time rememberin'
what that white dude said about mixing, about colors at war and
colors at peace, and then I put up some shit you ain't never gonna
see on top a Krylon can. After that I stop taggin' my work, and
that's tag enough. Everyone knows what's mine, the ship named
Detroit sinkin' into a river of garbage on the bridge, the fat black
Mona Lisa flippin' people off above the museum entrance. The

girls start smilin' at me at the matinee, flash me signs I don't flash back, smile again anyway. But Smak and Daze, they through. They follow me home from the show one day, bang on the door like to give Gran a heart attack. They say they don't like it, say a brotha gotta take credit for his work, gotta get creds for his crew, 'specially with all these punk-ass white boys out taggin'. But what they mean is they ain't got room for no renegade writer, arrogant bastard shitbombin' the fuck outta the city solo.

Scab absorbs other people's pain, and that's why I painted him over my bed where Ma used to be. Next to Scab are Ninja and Nefarius, and that's the wall Gran took to the art school in a picture, and that's why they wrote me a letter tellin' me not to worry about tuition and books. Gran's heart is bad, always been, and that's why I can't tell her I quit school. That, and she also got me in and told me every day to be strong, to show 'em I'm as good as they are. That's easy for her to say, but even if I believed it, there's a whole other part she don't know and won't understand, and that's the part about me seein' every day that I'm different, that I ain't got twenty-dollar pencils and hundred-dollar sweatshirts, that I don't know nothin' about Picasso or Wright and that what I do know don't mean nothin' in a place where they all know things different. So now I'm just a liar, hidin' out, layin' low. I find buildings to sleep in during the day, steal Fritos and Jolt from Tony's, or hit up the drive-thru chick for lunch when Gran thinks I'm at school. Sometimes I eat dinner with her before the dark starts me cravin' the wall, and I tell her I'm studyin' with some guys at school or that I'm goin' to the computer lab. She startin' to look at me funny, like Bloodhawk looks at the Rogue, with X-ray eyes.

I started out drawin' comic book characters, over and over and over. I never got tired. I stole Marvel and X-Men and Masters of the Universe comics, and I drew 'em on napkins and cardboard and all over the walls of the place Gran rents. When I was eight I used a picture to draw my mom over my bed, her long brown arms reachin' for me. When I was ten and she was still gone and I started to forget how she smelled and how she sounded, I got mad, and Gran slapped me hard after I painted needles comin' outta Ma's arms, but she cried when she did it 'cause she knew I was paintin' the truth, that Ma was never comin' back and that those needles would kill her, and by the time I was twelve I couldn't give a fuck if they did. Smak and Daze fools if they think they can make a family outta their crew, if they think a homey gonna stand up when your own mother don't.

But Smak and Daze don't let up, and this mornin' when I go to see the Black King—a piece so tight even the city ain't rushin' to buff it—somethin' twists inside me. The king's throat's slashed in red, and his eyes are black and he's smeared in globs of brown paint look like shit. Their tags are on it, the bent *Smak* and the bubble *Daze* I can hardly read but I can read, and below that it says, "Join the crew—BH." I wanna cry but I just get madder and start thinkin' about joining another crew so they can help me roll over the B-Hounds' stuff, keep my pieces safe on the wall. The sinking *Detroit* and Mona Lisa are already gone, but I go anyway, and see Smak and Daze bombed both walls over the whitewash with tags, claimin' territory, and they sprayed red X's over my phone booth rat and on all my Dumpster murals. They dissed *my* crew: Cyclops, Storm, Iceman, Kulan Gath. I start thinkin' about the pieces I'll do next: Cyclops cuttin' Smak to shreds with his eye-beam or Storm stabbin' a lightning bolt through his chest. But that's just stupid since my crew can't back me up when Smak and Daze and Metro and Booh come callin'. I go to the library and sit at a table and think about the bent *Smak* and the bubbled *Daze* and then I draw 'em on library scrap paper 'til it gets dark, 'til the security guard tells me to shove off and puts a five in my pocket, which lets me know I can buy some food straight up for a change and he's an angel and I'm gonna write him large somewhere someday, like Thor or Captain America. I sit at the Burger King and draw the *Smak* and the *Daze* some more, draw 'em 'til I can't stop, 'til I get the tilt and even the paint drips right, 'til even Smak and Daze won't know the difference.

Then I'm on, and I'm over the fence at the train station, and I'm hittin' the cars with shit so bad I gotta work to mess it up, and I sloppy-ass tag it *Smak* and *Daze* and hope the other nightcrawlers see it before they do. It feels good to piece even when it's bad, like a fix, but I'm still pissed my shit's been pulled down by fucks can't even throw up a clean tag. I'm a bomb tonight, change my style 'til it only gets worse and lay it all on them, start a diss explosion, an ass beatin' by the other crews who don't play up in here, who ain't havin' bullshit on the city canvas.

Outside the Town Apartments where the wall's been hit by every tagger in the city, I start to throw up some wack mural until I see it blinkin', a little red light on the front-door awning. I throw up my hood right before the camera flashes, and then I step to the side and watch it for a while. There's some old pallets stacked against the building, so I lean one against the wall under the camera, keepin' my face down, and before I climb up I pull the Minted Gold and the Crimson Red markers out the back-

pack. Then I do what I could do in my sleep: I tag the bent *Smak*
backward across the camera lens. After that I scout the overpasses
for more cameras, and then I throw up a rabid dog with crossed
eyes wearing a MCH cap and tag it big, the *Smak* and *Daze* pieced
on leashes around the dog's neck. This gonna bring out all the
Motor City Hoods, and I only wish I could be there to watch
'em roll up on Smak and Daze and their crew. Next I jump the
Junior Bombers' latest work with some trash, piece a JB tag with
a bloody sword through it over their train car mural after checkin'
for camera lights. Now the Hoods and Bombers gonna be huntin'.
After that I stop for the night; I know I gotta be cool. They ain't
gonna know it's me—the work's too sloppy—but without a crew
I *got* to be cool.

I hang out with Gran the rest of the night, watch some TV,
keep her company. She don't look so good, and she say she tired.

"The doctor say I need some test—"

"I love you, Gran." I say it 'cause I do and there's nothin' else
to say. I can't stand to look in her eyes and know that she can't
have nothin'—a healthy heart, a nice house, a grandson who can
make it in art school, who can plant his foot into the backward
system and step right anyway.

She leans into me, the ratty-ass sofa squeakin' like it's bein'
tortured, her hair stickin' up around her head like Apocalypse's in
the Grand Battle. "I love you too, baby."

"I got to tell you somethin'," I say, feelin' that old guilt blade
sawin' at my gut. "You can tell me about the doctor after. But I
gotta tell you now."

She hugs me hard and she says, "I know, baby. The school

called for you and they didn't say nothin' but I knew. I was just waitin' on you to tell me."

"I'm sorry, Gran."

"Maybe someday you'll go back, show them people how to draw."

"No," I say. "I'll find me a job, maybe at the Burger King."

"Well," she says, and hugs me again. "We'll figure it all out, baby. We'll figure it out."

She tells me her heart murmur's changed, somethin' about goin' from a blip-blip-blip to a blip-*blip*. The doctor don't like it, say she need some special test, and I say I'll take her and I will. I think for a long time about what it all means, Smak and Daze houndin' me, erasin' my soul in pieces, Gran gettin' sicker. Maybe it's time to stand up since I ain't real interested in gettin' arrested or killed right now. Maybe after I square up with the Bloodhounds I'll stay off the wall for a while. I'll throw a few more punches, make sure the other crews know the B-Hounds are frontin', stakin' all-out claim, and then I'll try to lay down.

"So you a bat now?" Gran asks. "Where you go all night?"

She looks at my wrist, checks for watches, and I know now she been in my room lookin' for iPods and Gameboys and all that, and I know all she ever find besides comic books and sketches are Krylon and Rustoleum.

"You be careful," she says before I can answer, and she squeezes my hand and I can't explain what I want to, how I always felt stupid in school and always feel good at the wall, a little high on fumes and pictures runnin' through my mind like a mad wind I gotta run to catch. Sometimes I wanna pick up the whole wall, to touch everything I pieced all at once so I can make it part of me, put it back in once it gets out. It'll be gone the next week, or the next day if it's on big-time turf, and that's what I wanna tell Gran. That the only time I'm real is when I'm doin' what I do better than anyone, that when I'm throwin' what's in my head onto the wall I'm alive. That the only time I'm happy is when I'm a criminal, and she ain't never gonna understand that.

A few days later Gran sets the paper next to my cereal bowl and taps her finger on a headline: "City Prosecutor Engaging in Smak-down." The article says the police have a "high profile" tagger in custody, someone cost the city over thirty grand in clean-up, a guy so arrogant he even tagged a security camera.

"Do you know this Theodore?" Gran asks.

"No," I say. "But he sound stupid."

"Sure does," she says, starin' at me through her frizzy hair. "Paintin' on walls with cameras all over."

"Yeah," I say. "I guess so."

I don't know how long Smak'll be in lockdown or if he already out on bail. Either way I'm a give myself one more night to finish the job, to take out as many B-Hounds as I can, to avenge the Black King and Cyclops and Nefarius. So when Gran falls asleep, I head out to the UA theater building on Bagley and look at how the punks done tore it up: lights ripped off the walls, velvet seats slashed, heads of sculptures bashed in. That's just wack, though I guess lots of folks on the city council don't think what I'm doin' is much better. Look like someone took a sledgehammer to the old vending machines, and with the broken heads and the empty paint cans it look like nothin' but death up in here. But I shake it off 'cause that's usually how it is when you piecin'—dark, empty buildings, dead cans layin' like bodies all over, the hissin' sound of huffers, addicts lookin' for that last high off a near-empty paint can. Sometimes the zombies come up and watch me, tell me how tight the piece is, but I know they can't even see straight, they just gonna try to beg or steal cans. Once in a while I throw 'em a dead one, but they too slow and pathetic to jump me for more.

After I scout the huffers, I climb the broken stairs to the twelfth floor where there's still some clean windows. I don't like writin' shit, but I know if I piece again for real the B-Hounds gonna roll over me. So I start hidin' messages in the piece just for fun, just to keep myself there. On the first window I draw a big-ass crooked beetle crushin' a tiny, bubbled Daze in his teeth, and the bent Smak is sliding out its asshole. I wanna do a Transformer on the second window, like Smak turning into a skeleton, but that's too close to my MO so I just throw up a nasty blob of colors, my arm snappin' like fire, and just as I start the bent *k* I hear the glass crunchin' on the floor behind me, and when I wake up my head's bleedin' and my paints gone, and the window above me say *Smak* and *Daze*. My right hand's fucked up, the fingers all bent, probably broken, and I figure they stomped my hand to put me off the wall.

When I get home I'm real quiet so I don't wake up Gran with her worried face and her blip-*blippin'* heart. My crooked fingers throbbin' and my head's still bleedin' and I dab at it a little with some toilet paper. But all that's nothin' compared to the paints—I lost twelve cans, two of 'em brand new, the red and gold of the B-Hounds. Maybe I should be glad they didn't kill me, though in a way they did; I know now I ain't never be able to write again, not in this city, not without a crew. I sit on the toilet seat with my head drippin' red into the sink, and for the first time since Ma left I cry like a baby. I get dizzy watchin' the red lines rollin' down the drain, and then I just get more tired than I ever been. I start to think for the first time about givin' up and wonder why I ain't never thought of it before. Ma did it, 'cause maybe she knew somethin' I'm just learnin', that it's easier to just quit. Maybe I'll leave this mess behind, take Gran down south where she grew up. Hell, I could get a job down there just as easy as here, maybe even piece a little to get the fix. When the bleedin' finally stops, I wrap my head in my old Superman towel and head for the kitchen where I can stare out the window at the blinking airplane tower and think about Louisiana, the gumbo vendors and the mist hangin' over the streets like Gran told me about. I can see myself there or in Georgia or on the moon; right now with my bloody head and my throbbin' hand I can see myself anywhere but here.

When I get to the kitchen, Gran's layin' on her stomach on the floor, and it look like she sleepin' and my heart starts poundin' and I yank the phone off the wall and dial 911 and the operator says, "Check her pulse" and "Do you know CPR?" and I touch her wrist but I can't tell and when I turn her over I see it all at once: the bruised throat and the blackened eyes and the bent *Smak* and the bubbled *Daze* sloppy 'cross her chest.

The 911 operator's yellin' through the phone but it ain't nothin' she can do for us now. When I take the carvin' knife off the wall to kill myself, I can't even hold it in my broken fingers so I scream and scream and scream until I'm on a stretcher and then I'm asleep and then I'm tellin' two detectives the whole story from a hospital bed, admittin' to the piecin' and taggin', and they say, "We're sorry, but we have no witnesses." They say Smak and Daze told 'em they been set up, say I killed Gran, say I stole their tags to get 'em arrested so I could collect her Social Security. "We found this in your pocket," they say, and hold up some library scrap paper full up with *Smak* tags. The detectives say, "We're tryin' to sort this all out."

But I ain't waitin' for them to sort it all out. I don't belong in Georgia or Louisiana or on the moon; for now I belong right here. I know what I gotta do. I'm a join the Bombers and the Hoods—hell, I got enough pictures in my head to join five crews, but it ain't the wall I'm after now.

RETREAT

As I wind my Expedition through the narrow roads looking for Registration, I feel anything but the peace and comfort I thought would somehow envelop me when I pulled off the highway and onto the gravel road leading to Tao Dai. Like everything else about me, my SUV feels *wrong*, out of place here, where overkill is discouraged, where treading lightly is rewarded, and where staying on the path is required. My anxiety turns to panic at road's end, where I see no signs and no turnaround. Is this a trick? A test of endurance, resourcefulness, and calm for new retreatants? Have they hidden the registration office to give us the opportunity to demonstrate sage, unconventional wisdom, or am I simply lost and, as usual, reading too much into my circumstance?

There is a light rapping on the passenger window, and I turn to see a stooped monk with a sour face pointing toward the narrow stretch of road I just drove. I click the remote button to lower the window, suddenly conscious of my shameless obsession with "lazy" technology, and ask how to get to the registration office. He continues to point down the road, his face twisting in on itself like a dried flower.

"But how?" I ask, and his eyes widen slightly. He continues to point down the road. "I can't turn around," I say, and he lets out a laugh, a choked, dead thing.

"Then don't," he says and walks into the surrounding woods, folding into the landscape like an apparition.

After making peace with the plan to steer backward down the narrow road toward the entrance—what choice do I have?—I turn to see a red Jeep framed in my rear window. Initially, I am relieved that someone else has made the same mistake, but then I realize that the person in the Jeep behind me will have to back up first and, as such, will have a front-row view of my own awkward, reluctant regression.

I'm here because of my failed novel. I'm here because I can't focus. I'm here because I don't like myself. We are living in "the New Age," one in which not liking yourself is tantamount to denouncing God, to being an ingrate, to requiring Prozac. When I leave, I will have either learned to like myself or made peace with the fact that I can't. Why don't I like myself? On a good day I'd say it's because I'm human, soft and sharp in all the wrong places, a pathetic sack of organic material with unrealistic hopes and expectations. On a bad day I'd say because of the karmic wheel on which what goes around comes around: I'm mean and judgmental, sometimes arrogant and self-serving, infinitely impatient with people who are just like me. If the day is particularly bad—the day my novel was rejected for the twelfth time, say—I'd say I don't like myself because I'm a bad writer.

Tao Dai is a Zen Buddhist monastery tucked into the Appalachian foothills, fifty-six miles from the nearest convenience store or fast-food restaurant. At orientation we learn that a flood has swept the foundation from under the trailer that formerly served as registration and that the sign directing visitors to the Seikan Center was later washed away too. Since I am wary by nature, forever worried about looking foolish or being on the wrong end of a joke, this explanation seems too simple to me. But I file it somewhere in the back of my mind, alongside other myriad and debilitating notions that I cannot shake, before making my way around the center and eyeing other retreatants curiously. I wonder why they are here, wonder if they too don't like themselves, wonder if they're even evolved enough to know it. Schedules are posted, and we are encouraged to sign up for as many classes as our stay here allows: yoga, journaling, *zazen, kinhin.* We are also encouraged to join the monks each morning at 3:30 for chanting.

"Who could sleep through *that?*" I say to the tall, thin, red-haired girl beside me, and she smiles before saying, "I'm sorry?"

"The chanting," I say. "Who could sleep through it?"

"Why would you want to?" she asks.

"Well, you wouldn't," I say. "It was a joke. Never mind."

"Hi," she says, offering her ghostly white hand. "I'm Sandi."

"Aren't you the red Jeep?" I ask, and she looks puzzled until I say, "I'm the black Expedition."

"Ah," she says. "Wasn't that awful?"

"Yeah. I don't even parallel park because I hate going backward."

"Our first trial," she laughs, and only then do I realize that she is pretty. "Still," she adds, waving her translucent hand in the air as if to erase the experience, "we are *so* lucky to be here."

I don't feel lucky, although I know I should. The monastery is beautiful—pagodas nestled in the woods, quiet gardens, labyrinthine footpaths—but we're lucky because we've been selected to attend this special week of "Quiet Therapies" based on a lottery the monks conducted after being inundated with requests. Other lucky retreatants I meet and with whom I will share a dormstyle pagoda are Phoebe, an anorexic who flinches easily; Monty and Clarice, an overweight middle-aged couple bent on publicly demonstrating their love; and Bernie, an automotive plant manager who works for his father-in-law and plays the banjo in a bluegrass band. My first impression of almost everyone here is that they're either clueless or damaged.

Each pagoda consists of five bedrooms, one bathroom, and a communal sitting space with a lamp, a futon, and large pillows scattered across the floor. My room is a cot, a dresser, three hooks on the wall, and an electrical outlet—the life source for my laptop and blow dryer. The first night we are encouraged to gather in the community room and introduce ourselves. I don't say that I'm a failed novelist who lives with her cat in a shoe-box apartment just north of Detroit. I say only that I'm a writer, and everyone oohs and aahs because the common definition of a writer is someone who has published at least one book. Sandi, a hair stylist from L.A., claims to hate pretension, says she wants to move to Brasilia and work with the World Wildlife Federation. Bernie oversees the production of two thousand windshield wiper motors each day in a small plant just outside Baton Rouge, and Phoebe, whose jaundiced eyes bulge from her sunken face, holds up the Rainbow Fish pillowcase that her kindergarten class has painted for her. She says she is from Boston; she says she has been sick. Monty and Clarice lean toward her in tandem, and Clarice touches Phoebe's brittle hair. They are lay ministers, they say, they've seen it all, and they're willing to talk to any of us about anything should we need an ear. "Thanks," we say. "Thanks."

After introductions Monty and Clarice regale us with stories of their first meeting, their first anniversary, their first home, each story punctuated with kisses and doe-eyed stares, as if remembered and told for the first time. They are dramatic, even ridiculous, and I can see that they are looking to pull everyone they meet into their act, to help bolster and underpin the ideal they have created. When they finish, Bernie launches into a great cover of the theme song from the *Beverly Hillbillies.* Phoebe sits on the floor biting her lip, her arms wrapped around her small body, elbows jutting at odd angles, and I watch Sandi as she watches Phoebe.

The mountain night is much cooler than the day, and as I lie shivering in my cot, listening to the muffled sighs of Monty and Clarice as their bulks shift heavily in the night, I consider the irony of my desire for solitude nestled beside my fear of loneliness. I think about the times I demanded to be in the driver's seat and then resented it, the times I demanded to be in the passenger seat and then felt vulnerable, my erratic dance with control.

In the morning I stare at the candle until I see two identical flames, and I don't know if I am hallucinating or if my eyes are tired. *Zazen,* or sitting meditation, begins at 5:30, and I did not sleep well. Everyone else appears calm, poised, but I am on the verge of inner panic: I cannot focus, and suddenly my mind rebels against order. It always has. As I attempt to force it into quiet, into emptiness, it doesn't assume its usual stance of stubbornness and restlessness but instead laughs at me. It tells me to feel awkward, out of place, ridiculous, alone. We are not supposed to look at one another—"This is not a competition," says Huyen Sa, the meditation monk—but instead allow the candle to light a path into ourselves, where we will see our own strengths and weaknesses, our own inner truths. This sounds to me at the same time brilliant and ludicrous.

Huyen Sa says he has asthma, that sometimes during deep meditation he struggles for breath without being consciously aware of it. If this occurs, we are not to intervene; we are to continue to sit with minds blank as white pages, faces as empty as prairie skies. "It is not as loud as a semitruck," he smiles. "Like everything else, you must accept it, relinquish it, and move beyond it."

Toward the end of class he reads affirmations, and we sit in lotus position, little Buddhas applying his words like a template over our lives. "Each person possesses his or her own perfectly enlightened nature," he says. "The water that flows down the mountain does not think that it flows down the mountain. The cloud that leaves the valley does not think that it leaves the valley." *The back that is aching does not think that it is aching, the ankle that is throbbing does not think that it is throbbing,* I think.

"In Buddha's country one arrives without taking even a single step," he says, and I smile at the ease with which my ankle dilemma has been dispensed. I am not missing the point, I realize as I sit on the wooden floor, my ankles on my thighs. I am, as usual, avoiding it.

At lunch Sandi says she heard me crying in my sleep. The walls are paper thin because they are made of paper. I say maybe it was Phoebe, who seems to be someone who would cry in her sleep, and Sandi says, "Maybe." She then tells me it's okay to feel like an alien, to be an alien. "It's a lonely trip," she says. "To Earth, I mean." She touches my right shoulder blade, and her hand feels strange to me, warming a place that until that moment I never considered, never thought of as a part of my body. Instinctively I bristle, but she doesn't remove her hand and I am simultaneously grateful for her understanding and incensed by her presumption. I could never touch someone like that, not even someone I know.

After lunch our journaling teacher, an author of two bestselling books about writing, tells us there is no good writing that is not honest writing. "Don't pick up the pen unless you're ready to tell the truth. Use it first to dig deep, then deeper, then all the way to the bottom. There are no doors. Go." I think about the truth, consider writing, *I'm a bad writer,* but instead write, *I'm not smart enough.* Then the irony falls on me like hail: I'm in a place where I cannot find definitive answers to my biggest questions, and I laugh aloud at my own stupidity, for not realizing it sooner. Everyone turns but the teacher, who stares through the window, absorbed in her own truths. I write that coming here is intellectually irresponsible, I write that I won't tell anyone, I write that suddenly this whole retreat feels pointless. Maybe I should be in a dusty garret somewhere poring over Stephen Hawking's *The Cosmos Explained* or wading through Joyce's *Ulysses.* Maybe I should be compiling a genealogy to track my bloodline to a long-lost ancestor who can unlock the mystery of my mental and

emotional malaise—a schizophrenic aunt chained in a dank base-
ment, a great-grandfather whose intellectual capacities were taxed
by a square peg and a round hole. *Who's back there?* I write. *Who
gave me green eyes? Who gave me a propensity for self-hatred? Who
gave my parents my inherited burden?* After class I flip through *Zen
Keys,* a book by Thich Nhat Hanh that the teacher is promoting,
and read, "When its roots are cut, the tree is felled," and I wonder
if gnarled and twisted roots can ever produce healthy trees.

My mother was institutionalized for depression when I was ten;
that's what they did back then. She would cut half my bangs, or
peel half a carrot, or dust half the coffee table before settling into
the wingback chair and crying over the sad movies featured in
her mind. "You're halfway there, Greta," my father would say as
she vacuumed the carpet or diced potatoes, as if she didn't know,
as if the stoplight and the projection screen in her head hadn't
simultaneously blinked on. We would visit her on Sundays, and
my dad would hold her hand as she ate half a plum, and after a
while I saw something akin to the movies in my mother's head:
two sad people, one who was crazy and one who refused to believe
it. I know my roots: I've grown from the insanity and denial that
are my foundations, and sometimes cutting them seems worth the
risk of felling the tree.

After dinner I go to the Seikan Center for a two-hour hatha yoga
class. Sha Nin, the instructor, is lethargic, and his bones crack
and his body rebels when he bends to kneel. "This is not a competition," he says, and I realize that this is the collective mantra
of the Tao Dai, a concept the monks feel they must impart to

their guests, mostly Americans who have come into their monastery from the grip of capitalism, of materialism, of competition. "Don't go into pain," he admonishes. But I do. I take each stretch further than I should, refuse to bend my knees, hold positions too long because I *do* look at the others, because I have to succeed where they fail, because I must prove to myself that I am better than they are in order to truly believe I might be almost as good.

Sha Nin's yoga mat is frayed at the edges, his sitting pillow is dingy, the color of tobacco-stained teeth, and his gray sweatshirt has a long, peninsular stain cascading down the front. As if reading my mind, Sha Nin kneels on his mat, the pitch of his popping spinal bones rising like xylophone keys being struck by a mallet, and says, "There is no enlightenment outside of daily life." *Then what am I doing here,* I wonder, and I peek at the others, who appear to have moved easily beyond the contradiction of their situations. I sit cross-legged, pulling my ankles back toward my hips until I feel pain in the muscles of my thighs.

"You are where you are today," he says as we move from child to cat pose, from cat to frog, from frog to pigeon. "Honor your body." An hour into class it is clear that Phoebe is a regular yoga practitioner, but Monty and Clarice are sweating profusely in their matching flannel sweatsuits, and Bernie is snoring on his mat. The other students don't appear to notice, but Sha Nin does. He tells us to lie on our backs, arms at our sides; he covers each of us with a thick, decorative blanket. Slowly and methodically, he tucks the blankets under our chins, covers our feet, tells us to close our eyes. I hear the clap of a CD being inserted into the player, the whir of the disc as it spins into place, then the sound of water spilling from the sky.

"Consider," Sha Nin says, "spring rain waters all plants equally, and yet the flowering branches are long or short," and I want to say, "But what about the sun, the soil, the roots?"

We lie on our mats for thirty minutes, or forty minutes, or more. We lie on our mats until we are all asleep, and none wants to return when Sha Nin rouses us. We sit up, hands joined palm to palm in *gassho,* in expression of the "One-Mind," and we bow to the master. I hike to the pagoda feeling both rested and exhilarated, my desire to practice yoga overtaking my desire to write, for there is little failure in yoga.

Our journaling homework is to write about frustration, about thwarted effort. Although I immediately feel capable—after all, I'm nothing if not a frustrated writer—I sit on my cot and write about parking tickets and sold-out ball games. I write about burnt dinners and faulty alarm clocks. I can't bring myself to write about the amount of energy I've wasted on impotent yearning, believing I was madly in love with men I knew I couldn't have, even knowing I wouldn't want them once I could. I can't write about how much time I've spent imagining the perfect relationship, or that I sometimes imagine the perfect man hitting me, or that I sometimes imagine halfway through the fight the red light will blink on and I'll tune out. Sometimes I imagine the perfect man leaving me for another woman, or leaving me for another man, or leaving me simply because he can no longer tolerate my lunacy and denial, and the crying jag that follows is euphoric. But I don't write about that, or about my agent's last phone call, or about my half-ironed school shirts. I write about the late bus, the lost keys, the burnt chips.

My father lived in his head as much as my mother, finishing her half-eaten pie or weeding the other half of the flowerbeds, dispensing with the physical evidence that threatened his pathological desire for normality. He always said my mother would get better if she believed she would, and he spent many hours wandering the antiseptic halls of the asylum espousing the validity of this theory, explaining to her that it was she who created her own reality.

My mother never bought the theory—maybe she never heard him, or maybe she heard only half of what he said—but it worked on me in a convoluted and insidious way, and I started to create my own realities early on. As a writer I could escape into worlds of my own making. I could swim in someone else's life for a while, become a girl who was rich, one who hated her parents because they loved her too much, or a character so burdened and afflicted that his life made mine look easy. It is at first empowering, the ability to become someone else, but when it becomes addicting, when anybody's life feels better than your own, you realize that you, like your father, have manipulated the theory to reconcile the life you have with the life you want, to fool yourself into believing you are happy.

The next morning I sleep in, and at lunch Monty and Clarice, attached eternally at the hands, approach me in their yellow jogging suits to say I missed an inspired *zazen* class; they ask if I'd like them to wake me the next day at five. They are too cheerful, their clothes are too bright, and their happiness—real or imagined—makes me angry. I want to scream at them, I want to tell them they are pathetic and self-deluded, I want to cry, but instead I say, "Sure, thanks."

In journaling, the teacher asks if anyone would like to share his or her thoughts on frustration, and a tall blonde woman who looks as if she'd been constructed by a team of plastic surgeons raises her hand. I expect the teacher to call her Bambi or Tammi, but instead she says, "Madge." The woman opens the decorative cover of her leather-bound journal and reads: "The world just keeps moving. It closes around our thoughts and actions and pain, compensates and overcompensates until what we do or think or feel fills a new gap the world has created for it." She stops, takes a deep breath, shakes her head as if having a silent argument with someone, then continues: "It doesn't matter what happens to us— the world smoothes it over, evens it out, wears it down, makes it seem right whether it is or not." She sits down, and the rest of us look around, waiting for someone else's lead. The teacher thanks her and begins an encouraging round of applause. Madge turns red, Madge smiles shyly, Madge tells us she's been medicated for depression. She says she was in the third car of a forty-seven-car pile-up after an oil tanker jackknifed and dumped its load on Interstate 20 in Texas. She has undergone eighteen reconstructive surgeries over the past five years; she says she is startled each time she encounters a mirror. My burnt dinners suddenly feel small, even the failed novel. I don't know how my mother's insanity stacks up, but then I hear it rising from the back of my mind, quiet and commanding: *This is not a competition.*

Bernie raises his hand, reads about how he gets blamed when a line shuts down, when the union wins a valid grievance, when the company loses a contract. "Hell," he says, "one of the guys passes gas and I get blamed for the smell." Everyone laughs, even Bernie, but he is clearly hurt by his father-in-law's meanness and oppression. He cannot read between the lines of his words; he cannot see that his father-in-law does not like him, that he'd be more comfortable in a blue collar, that he's too humane to run a greed-inspired venture. "What do you think you should do?" says the teacher, and Bernie shrugs. Tonight's assignment, she says, looking from Madge to Bernie: "How do we live through it?"

How do we live through it? I type, and then I stare at the blinking cursor on the laptop screen. I eat three of the chocolate chip cookies I brought. I assume several yoga postures. I glance around my tiny, drab room and understand that it has been decorated in antidistraction themes. I eat two more cookies, I tell myself I will be honest, and I write:

> *How do we live through it? How do we survive the impossible to survive? That's why we're either clueless or damaged, in denial or crazy. How else can we live? And how can we possibly like ourselves when we live this way? I don't have it all figured out, and I'm not naive enough to believe these monks do, either. They've just learned to give in to the current, to eddy with the water around the rocks of pain and heartache, even to disappear into the depths of the whirlpool. They've given in. Who am I not to give in? So what if I've lost pieces of myself? Who am I, anyway?*

I eat two more cookies. I stare at my stomach. I slap my forehead. I write,

> *My mother was weak and helpless, and she abdicated her duty*

to me because it was an impossible job. Can anyone stand be-
tween a child and an avalanche? Can anyone pull you from the
fiery abyss or the tornado's eye, things sprung from the minds of
gods? We are such small things in the face of calamity, really.
We are nothing. Why do we tell ourselves otherwise? We live
through it by lying, or by convincing ourselves that we're not
important, that nothing we do is of consequence, that nothing,
nothing, nothing, nothing, nothing, nothing, nothing matters.

At 5:00 AM I open the door to find Monty and Clarice, puffy-eyed
and smiling, waiting for me in their khaki ensembles. We walk the
narrow path to the *zendo,* Monty pulling Clarice up the incline
as we parade single file, and when we arrive we find four students
already seated on the hard wooden floor, eyes lost in meditation.
Huyen Sa says his arthritis is acting up; we will do *kinhin,* or walking meditation, today. "Place the hands in *shashu,*" he says, "palms
over the chest and elbows out in a straight line. We will move
clockwise around the room, taking a half step for each full breath,
slowly, smoothly, and noiselessly. We will not drag the feet. We
will walk straight ahead; we will always turn to the right." He
begins, and we follow, little ducks, odd brides, lost souls. I look
at the others, eyes open, each step important, overblown, pro-
nounced. We look like automatons and that is, I guess, the idea.
Give the body an easy task so that the mind can focus on something more crucial than locomotion. It is difficult to convince
your mind to forget what your body is doing, to suppress the frustration of what feels like a painfully slow, meaningless enterprise.
But I am determined to make use of the session, to be less cynical

about my approach, to make some sort of progress, and so I move and I think, I move and I think. After three revolutions I decide to let go of the novel: I'll write another one. After five revolutions I am uncharacteristically kind to myself: Would I really want to be anyone else? During our ninth revolution I watch the folds in Clarice's shirt shift as she sways in front of me, and I am suddenly sad. Why can't I be nicer? How can the torn seam on her shirt make me want to cry when ten minutes earlier I wanted to scream at her, to puncture the illusion she needs to survive? The mysteries of our emotions are too complex to unravel, even when given a free mind to contemplate them. How do we live with them? How do we survive them?

For lunch we have rice, fruit, and water. I'm thinking about my chocolate chip cookies, I'm thinking about my writing assignment, I'm thinking about Clarice's shirt. I'm thinking about anything but my rice, fruit, and water. Even after practicing *kinhin* for an hour, I am not mindful of the present but instead obsessed with the past and the future. I bite into a strawberry. I pay attention: it is sour and coarse. The rice is mealy, overcooked but for one raw grain that I've bitten into my molar. The brown sauce is thick and sweet. There was thought put into this meal: the firm fruit, the soft rice, the sweet sauce, the water that washes it all away.

Sandi sits beside me and prays over her food, and this takes me by surprise, makes me see that I am typically more angry than grateful, more selfish than selfless, and I realize suddenly how weary I've grown of my constant companions, anger and resentment. *Get over it,* I tell myself, *play the hand you've been dealt.*

After lunch Monty and Clarice trundle off to the pagoda for a nap, and Sandi and I stroll the Path of Reflection toward one of the monastery's quiet gardens. She tells me she's going to quit her job, move to South America, and I believe her. She is forceful and confident, traits I recognize in myself as much as I do Phoebe's fear and self-hatred, Bernie's denial, Monty and Clarice's desire to construct a life that in reality eludes them. "I'm happy for you, Sandi," I say. "Write to me." She says she will, and I'm already looking forward to her first letter, perhaps for the vicarious thrill of a well-spent life.

We cross the stone bridge and enter the garden to see Bernie sitting on a boulder, staring into the lotus pond, cradling his banjo. There is no doubt that other guests would complain about the raucous sound of bluegrass music in the quiet garden, but I don't want to broach the topic because he looks so sad.

"That's one beautiful banjo," says Sandi as we sit on the rocks near his feet.

Bernie lays the banjo on his lap, contemplates it. "Yeah," he says. "This banjo's my best friend goin' on twenty years. I played it at my wedding. Played it at my brother's funeral."

I wonder about that, about crossing boundaries: banjoes at weddings, banjoes at funerals. But then I wonder whose boundaries I'm crossing. As if reading my mind, Bernie says, "He asked me to. He knew he was dying."

"That must have been beautiful," I say. "That must have been hard."

"No," says Bernie. "It's easy to give people what they want when it's something you like to give, when it's something that makes you feel better. It was a lot harder coming here. He asked me to do that too. I'm here on his ticket."

"What an incredible gift," says Sandi. "A week to rest and meditate, to calm your spirit."

Bernie shakes his head. "Too much thinking," he says. "Sometimes it's better not to know."

"It only *feels* better not to know," says Sandi.

"Right there," says Bernie, stabbing the air as if to puncture Sandi's words. "What's wrong with feeling better? Ignorance is bliss? Hell, I'll take bliss any day."

"Sounds like it's too late," I say.

"Amen," says Bernie in a mock preacher tone, "I've eaten from the Tree of Knowledge."

"Doesn't taste very good, does it?" I ask, and Bernie sighs, hugs his banjo, wipes his eyes.

The writing teacher does not ask us to share our thoughts on surviving the impossible. Instead, she distributes a wild assortment of writing implements: gel pens, mechanical pencils, ballpoints, fine lines, markers, bright crayons. She distributes neon-colored posterboards and tells us to write the word *thoughts* across the top. "Small paper equals small thoughts," she says. "Big paper . . . well, you see where this is going. Change writing instruments if your thoughts require it. Don't sign your name. Go."

I choose a fine line. I tell myself I hate this. I think about Bernie, crying over his banjo, then I think of my dad, crying over my mother, and then I think of my mother, crying over everything. Then I write,

*My thoughts are not my friends, and I should never be alone
with them. They have sharp edges, razor teeth, and dark inten-
tions. They are powerful and should not be played with. They
should come with warnings. I think my mother's did: Caution.
Curve ahead. Loose rock. She always stepped back from the
edge, but what she did after that might not be called living.*

The teacher walks by. She runs her finger under the words *my
mother's*, whispers "Your thoughts" and keeps walking, running
her finger along other neon posters, whispering to other writers.

I take a happy face pencil. I write,

*Maybe my mother's thoughts are my thoughts, maybe my fa-
ther's thoughts are my thoughts, how do I know? Maybe I can't
collect my mind because I don't have one; maybe I can't concen-
trate because it requires the impossible: reconciling an inheritance of conflicting ideas about what it means to live, to love, to
work, to grow. Maybe I don't know what I think. Goethe says
the greatest truths can only be expressed dramatically. Maybe
Goethe's thoughts are my thoughts. Maybe I need more drama
in my life. Maybe that's why I'm here, ironically, seeking drama
in a vacuum where even our leaders are damaged or broken,
small men with big demands and strange ways of expressing
them. Why do I seek their approval? Why do I seek anyone's
approval? Why do I blame my parents for my insecurities, for
my obsessions, for my shame? Because they were trapped in a
perpetual present of sad movies and half-finished tasks, lost in
worlds of their own design, oblivious to a daughter who tried to
save them? Who in their right mind rejects a savior?*

Then my mind cracks open, and I see the impossibility of it all, and I write, *Who among us even recognizes one?*

Phoebe does not show up for yoga, and I am so distracted by her absence, so certain she is ill, that I assume the postures only half-heartedly. Later Monty and Clarice will tell me in confidence about an unexpected opening at a world-renowned eating disorder center, about strings pulled and bribes offered by Phoebe's gold-encrusted father, and I will rethink the life of the rich girl who hates her parents because they love her too much.

Huyen Sa has been hospitalized following an asthma attack, and the young monk assigned to conduct the final *zazen* class is formal, rigid, serious, healthy. His eyes do not dance, his voice does not reflect the weary experience of Huyen Sa's, and his demeanor is authoritative rather than nurturing. Hien Tu takes us through twenty minutes of *zazen,* ten minutes of *kinhin;* he taps our shoulders with a *kyousaku* stick when our eyes close, he demands equal distance between us as we traipse slowly around the dark *zendo*. We feel awkward and scattered when Hien Tu interrupts our meditations, taps our feet to control the rotation. Suddenly I miss Huyen Sa's labored breathing, his disdain for schedules, his whispered affirmations; suddenly I realize that orchestrated perfection, my habitual approach to life, is a tiring and empty enterprise.

The writing teacher has compiled everyone's thoughts into a parting gift, a scroll tied with gold ribbons. "We are made poetry by our pathologies," she says, quoting Thomas Moore. "Our lives are stories that generate pure wisdom, sage advice." We untie our scrolls, we sit silently, we read:

> *Writing can be a distraction from thinking, from deep personal reflection. How can we reconcile the two?*

> *I've been craving a hamburger all week, yet once I leave here I'll no longer want one. Who said, "Desire that fades with delay is not holy desire?"*

> *I've spent the first half of my life hating my parents, the second half forgiving them. Why am I giving them so much and myself so little?*

> *Three phone calls, three fatal accidents. I unplugged the phone, but people called anyway.*

> *My life isn't exciting—I don't have a great job or a nice house or even a girlfriend at present—but I'm happy. I'm optimistic. Something always floats down the river and climbs up the shore.*

> *I told my wife I'd kill myself if she left. She left, and I'm dead, but I'm still eating and sleeping and shitting and crying and writing.*

> *I can't get my feet out of the mud, so I've decided the mud isn't such a bad place to be.*

I always think something incredible is about to happen, and it always does.

Since my husband died I refuse to eat alone, so I look forward to my meals. When there's no one to eat with, I look forward to fasting.

Who in their right mind rejects a savior? Who among us even recognizes one?

As I read people's thoughts, their reflections upon life's pivotal moments, I understand that we are all damaged, that we all live under a smoke screen of our creation, and that most of us don't like what we see when the fog is lifted. It is hard to be honest, so instead we pretend to be smart, or happy, or strong. And it's tiring. I decide that it's sometimes all right to feel inadequate or to dislike myself, but it's never all right to punish myself.

I unplug the blow dryer, I zip the laptop into its case, I throw my luggage into the back of the truck. Sandi drifts out of the woods and stands before me with her palm out, and I hand her the notebook page on which I've scrawled my address.

"I mean it," I say, and she nods.

"What now?" she asks, and I say, "The next novel. You might be in it."

"I'm five-foot-eight," she says, "I hate peanut butter, and I'm a bitch in the morning."

"I know who you are."

"Send me excerpts," she says. "There's not much night life where I'm going."

Monty and Clarice start loading the Saturn beside me, and I give them my remaining chocolate chip cookies. They tell me they're headed to a mission in Mexico, where for a month they will harvest corn, mend fences, and clean cow stalls. They are still holding hands, even as Monty dips into the bag and places a cookie into Clarice's waiting mouth, and I believe, at least at that moment, that they have lost the boundary between them, that they are happily, truly, and inexorably one.

I look for Bernie, but he's already left. "He wanted to make the night shift," says Sandi. "He went back to the plant, back to his father-in-law, back to someone else's dream."

I shake my head. "He's eaten from the Tree of Knowledge," I say, and Sandi smiles.

As I exit the monastery gates, I feel calmer than when I entered, even though I am again facing the unexpected. I don't know what I'm going back to—a phone call from my agent, a letter from my father, a strengthened will to grow, to write, to live—but I know it can't be the same thing I left. Sometimes the most obvious lessons take the longest to learn, but I now know that the roads leading to the past have been hopelessly colored by time, forever altered on the skewed maps of our memories. Perhaps my initial aversion to a backward journey stemmed from my unconscious knowledge of its impossibility. What can I do, then, but make the weighty, conscious decision to travel roads that lead to the future instead of the past, to break free of the toxic pull of history, to lean forward, forward, forward into the luminous arms of the unknown?

Call me what you like, I say, and usually they come up with every-thing from the obvious to the creepy, which under the circum-stances should be expected. Some of them call me Red because of my signature hair, auburn strands charging the air like flames. But in the end *Bambi, Candy, Tammy*—names that are both childish and suggestive—are the top choices, and the doctors and teachers and executives imagine they are novel and clever with their winks and their crooked smiles, as if we've stumbled on an inside joke. Some call me Gladys or Mabel, and once I was Ernestine. *My mother's name,* he'd said. *I bet you think that's weird.* I shrugged. I let them imagine they are novel and clever or even weird; I let them imagine they are Spider Man or Bill Clinton; I let them imagine they are pounding their mothers in cheap motels, mon-ster trucks, red leather backseats. That's my job.

Don't judge me.

That's my opening line. Not *Don't judge me* but *Call me what you like.* It's an icebreaker, and it gives me an idea of what type of guy this is, what he needs, if I should be careful. I'm looking for the guys who pick baby names, the Lulus and the Brittanys, 'cause they're in and out in fifteen minutes, though they also tend to be the talkers, the ones who regret cheating on their wives, who say they've never done anything like this before, who say *you're a nice girl how did you end up here you should come to my church*. This is the classic penance, the belief in forgiveness from the higher power if you drag another soul along. I glance at my watch, make like a shrink when I say, *Time's up.*

It's the salesmen who jerk me around, who try to renegotiate the price afterward, as if the service comes with some sort of guarantee. He can't come because the Stewarts walked out on a million-dollar deal—*fuck-that-goddamn-Kathleen-Stewart* he screams at the back of my head, plunging and slamming, my hair yanked through his fat smelly fists—and his anger and frustration are my fault. The real estate guys and the Porsche salesmen call me Zoe or Chantal or Winona, after their customers, their secretaries, the owners' daughters who don't avert their eyes, who stare at them like people stare at me, like they smell shit. It's a good thing to know what people think of you; it's a good position from which to operate. Listen, I don't kid myself about anything.

There are the sleek, slick guys who look like movie stars; they are young and rich and confused about their feelings, their futures, their sexuality. Word will sweep like wildfire through the country club if they can't get it up with Johanna and Devon, if they don't somehow silence the urges that bloom in their tennis shorts when they watch Kyle stroking the head of his polo mallet. This is what they say to me as I feel their heartbeats pulse through the flesh in my mouth, as I work their small cocks into something more, make them believe they're not gay because my job is to fulfill fantasies. There are the meaty truckers who broadcast our sex over CB radios, the heavily inked bikers—knives and lions and Satan writhing across their backs—who want to fuck on their Harleys, the men who've come to realize they're married to ugly, distant strangers. When I dropped out of college, when I stopped reading Yeats and writing bad poetry, I thought about keeping a tally of the men I'd had, sending an employment journal to my perfect parents. But my clients all blended one into the next, clichés so real and boring I lost count.

So I've seen pretty much every type. One of my regulars is a priest. I figure it's better he slide his holy cock up my ass than up the altar boys'. The fact is, he's the only customer I've ever really admired, offered a discount when the heat strikes, when he's on his knees weighing the options. He faced his demons full on and did what he had to do, didn't put himself first, I don't think. I actually thought about a punch card for him, nine visits and the tenth one free or something like that, but of course this is a paperless business. I think about that priest sometimes and want to ask what parish he leads, not that I'd saunter into the House of God some Sunday morning in my halter and heels, but you never know, right? Do you want to know what the priest calls me? Mary.

A lot went through my mind when that priest first mounted me, and this is unusual as I'm mostly cued in to the client, moaning after a particularly deep thrust or begging for more when they slow down, trying to speed things along. But I'd been raised Catholic and left the church after realizing it was all smoke and mirrors and threats, left my Holy-Roller hypocritical parents in a big way, and I was trying to find a name for our encounter: irony? vengeance? destiny? But there was no winner in that dark red motel room, and that made the naming impossible. When the priest came, he thanked me, and I covered my naked breasts as he peeled the bills from a thick wad in his fist, and I still think about the stupid, stupid thing he did, showing all that green to a pro.

Why am I telling you this? Because tonight's john is different. He does not call me Candy or Zoe or Mary. He drives slowly, jerks off as he tails me down Monroe, tells me to get into the fuckin' car. He'll be a rough one, and I grow a little excited by the prospect of something *different*, though I do recalculate my prices before I even touch the rusted chrome handle of his beat-up Monte Carlo.

Call me what you like, I say as I smile and slide into the passenger seat. *Shut the fuck up,* he says. *How much?* I ramble off the price list, and he says, *One of everything.* I laugh to myself: even if he can afford it he can't handle it. He's bald and fat and has an ancient tattoo stretched across his biceps, an old rocker, a greaser in a leather vest. *You got a place?* he asks. I don't take johns to my place since some of us girls got together—I guess you could call it a co-op—and bought out the Serendipity, a decrepit motel in Bakersfield. We don't have a pimp since our operation is small and fringe, since the big shooters haven't yet figured out just how popular the outskirts are, though we have Nina, Cicely's daughter, who is two hundred pounds of muscle and attitude. She sits at the front desk with one hand on the telephone and the other on the trigger, a dyke praying for a john to go off. *Yeah,* I say, *the Serendipity on Lexington—*

No, he says, as if suddenly remembering something. *I know a place,* and I say, *All right,* and start watching street signs, making a road map in my head. He takes Monroe out to Nathan, Nathan to Farley, where it curves around the river and ends in a blighted industrial complex: an old stamping plant, a defunct tool-and-die shop, abandoned warehouses. *Where is this place?* I ask calmly, though I shift my purse onto my lap, note its heft, and relax a little. *I don't wanna be seen,* he says, *I got a reputation.* I ask him what he does and he says, *Shut the fuck up, okay?* In my mind I call him John because he is generic in one way: a loser posing as a winner, a tough guy in a twenty-year-old car with a prostitute heading toward the slums and pretending he's got something worth protecting.

We pull up to the old tire plant, its windows cracked and broken, a hundred jagged smiles facing me when I look up. *There's nothing here,* I say, but he ignores me and gets out of the car. *Inside,* he says, *I wanna to do it in here.* I follow him into the plant, my right hand in my purse, fingers wrapped around the butt of my .38. My heart's slamming; the thought of the narrow barrel, the cold metal, the thin trigger. I've never killed anyone, but you're fooling yourself if you don't think that any one of us can. I think about the promise I made to myself when I first got into the business: that if I ever had to kill someone, I'd keep it quiet, slip out of town, swim deep, and then resurface as something bright and shiny and new. But I tell myself that that won't happen, not tonight.

The plant is dark and smells like oil and dirt, like diesel. John snaps on a Mag-Lite that throws a wide beam across the floor where pieces of glass wink and sparkle in its wake. He moves into the dark and I stay by the door; there are no cars outside, but I'm no fool. I keep my hand on the gun. *Let's do it in the car,* I say, but he keeps walking, his feet shuffling over glass, cardboard, the detritus of a long-dead dream. *Are you fucking deaf?* he says. He shines the light on a conveyor belt and then, as an afterthought, flashes it across the inside of the plant, either to show me no one else is there or to assure himself. Rats skitter through the beam and he shakes his head and laughs as if they're funny, as if there's nothing stranger than finding rats in an abandoned building. *Here,* he slaps the conveyor belt hard and the mechanical underbelly groans. *Git on up.*

This is going to cost more, I say, looking around to show him why, thinking he'll get pissed and leave me there or get pissed and come after me. Either way. *Okay,* he says. *Sure. No problem. I hear you're worth it.* I ask who recommended me and again he shakes his head and laughs. The bikers, I think, the guys who want to do it on bikes and in bathrooms, in fields or truck beds—anywhere but at the motel. He seems unfazed, in control, so I walk toward him, tell him to take off his pants to see if he'll be dominated. *I'm paying you extra,* he says, *you take off my goddamn pants.* He sets the flashlight on the belt so it spotlights me, but all I'm thinking about are his two free hands. My own hand is still on my purse; I want him to try something and I don't. I move fast, practically run at him and force my tongue into his mouth as I claw at his belt buckle with my free hand. The element of surprise. If he's going to hurt me, I figure it'll be now. But he doesn't. As I slide my tongue in and out of his mouth, I slip the gun from my purse to the conveyor belt, behind the light, close but not close enough. He moans as I lower his pants, as I slip my fingers between his sweaty gut and his tightly cinched underwear, as I knead his doughy flesh. His erection is instantaneous; I push him against the belt so I'll be close to the gun, and when I kneel to take him into my mouth, he stiffens, his cum spraying my chest and arm. *I won't need the gun,* I think, almost laugh, and when I stand to face him, he punches me in the mouth. I stagger a little but don't fall—I can take a punch—and I lunge toward the belt, my hand striking the gun on the first try, too hard, pushing it off the other side. *What the fuck?* he yells, shining the light into the darkness beyond the belt, at the floor where he'd heard a metallic thud. *What was that?* I shrug. *You want it rough?* I ask, rubbing my jaw. *You gotta tell me in advance. That costs more too.* He laughs. *Where's the fun in that? C'mere.* He reaches toward me, stepping out of the pants pooled at his feet. *I'll take off your clothes. I'll be nice. I promise,* he says. *How 'bout you hit me?* I jump into the punch like a jackhammer, like a pitcher winding up, my fist crashing into his temple, and he falls back against the belt smiling. He can take a punch too. *Okay, we're even,* he says. *I was just mad at the expense and everything, that I wasn't gonna get my money's worth. C'mon now. I got paid today, I'll give you the whole goddamn check. Just gimme what I need, gimme a little more time. That's all I'm asking.*

He holds up his hands in surrender, taps the belt three times, as if calling a dog to jump onto a sofa, and I nod as I watch his dark form, as I climb up. *Okay,* he says, *if I get too rough you say so. I like to have some fun, that's all. You just let me do the work for a while.* I lie down on the belt, its cracked rubber edges digging into my back, and look for a glint or gleam of the gun's barrel on the floor to my right. John places the flashlight above my head and when he pushes my dress up and bends my knees toward my chest, the beam, deflected off my thigh, fans out to display a

wider section of the cement floor and there's the gun, practically
on display. I lower my knee a little and John pushes it back; the
belt whines as he climbs up and straddles it, bends over to force
his fleshy face into my crotch.

The .38 seems shinier than ever and as he licks and pants, I
think about buying a new gun, a dark gun, a smaller gun I can
hide . . . where? He tears my dress open at the chest—that'll cost
him—and squeezes my breasts hard, as if trying to pop them, as
if he's trying to get more enjoyment out of them than they can
offer. The flashlight beam above me burns my head, and I reach
up to move it slightly, to touch the metal shaft as John's tongue
races inside me, as if he's cleaning me. His breath quickens, and I
realize I haven't said anything in a while so I groan a little, tell him
how good it is, and he squeezes my breasts harder, and I whisper,
Easy, and he starts banging on the conveyor belt beneath me with
his fists. *Goddammit, it ain't working,* he screams, *you ain't into me.
Just shut up if you can't be into me.* It's not easy to be convincing
when stretched out on a conveyor belt in a dark tire plant, pinned
by a nutcase while hiding a gun. *C'mon,* I say, and smile, spread
my knees wider, but he's distracted, frustrated, holding his limp
dick and looking like he wants to break something. *It's this place,* I
say, reaching forward to touch his arm. *I'm into you, but I could be
more into you somewhere else.* He shakes his head. *Here!* he shouts,
sprouting from between my legs like a volcano, his face slick with
me, his hands crawling up my body toward my neck. *Goddamn
you,* he says, *what the fuck am I paying you to argue with me?* His
hands circle my neck; I can feel a thick-banded ring gouging my
skin. *Easy, baby,* I say as his hands tighten around my throat. *Easy,*
I whisper until I grow dizzy and look at the floor; he follows my

gaze, sees what I see, squints in the direction of the gun, smiles wide as my breath gurgles and my hands close around the base of the flashlight and he squeezes my neck until my breath comes in desperate squeaks, until the metal shaft arcs through the thick air and crashes into his naked skull. John tips back, slamming onto the belt, and I shine the flashlight onto his face. He's gasping, lying in the blood pooling around his head. *Sorry, baby,* I say, and I slip the ring off his sweaty finger.

Maybe it's not appropriate to think about such things at times like these, and maybe it's even less appropriate to think about how appropriate something is at times like these, but Mag-Lite is a damn good product, still shining after a hard blow to a solid object. I use the light to gather up my purse and the gun and his wallet, leave John spread across the conveyor belt and moaning in the dark. I think about slashing his tires, stealing his car since he'll come looking for me either way. Instead I call Nina on my cell and ask her to come out to the warehouse district. While waiting, I walk along the river in the dark, worried that the crazy fuck will tear out of the warehouse and come after me if he sees the light, and when I see Nina's Bronco up the road, I fling the flashlight and the empty wallet far into the black, black water.

"Jesus Christ," she says when I slide into the passenger seat. "Where is he?"

"I don't know," I say. "He threw me out of the car."

"I told you only at the motel. You see him again, you tell me. I'll slice that motherfucker up and down."

Nina likes to destroy things; Nina would have killed John, and at that moment, as I stare at my bruised throat and my bloody lip in the passenger-side mirror, I'm tempted to let her. Instead I go home and soak John out of my hair and my skin, consider and forget calling my parents, feel the heat and the sounds and the smells once again closing in on me. When I have too much time to think, I wonder how long it will be before the downtown pimps realize the johns they've lost are at the Serendipity, before they come with fists and bullets and fire. At one time this would have excited me, a drama fix shot through my veins, death's foreplay. But tonight I didn't feel a rush, and thinking that a stupid fuck who couldn't even state his needs almost killed me only makes me tired.

The next night I stay home, and Nina calls to say someone's been by three times looking for me, says he'll be back, says he doesn't want anyone else. I ask if he has a big crack in his skull, and she laughs, describes a guy so bland it could be anyone but John. I'm still tired the following night when I drive to the Serendipity, when I climb the fire escape stairs and crawl through an upstairs window. I'll take the walk-ins—I'm not hoofing it tonight—and I tell Nina to send up only the Lulus and the Brittanys so I can sleepwalk the routine. My first customer opens the door slowly, shyly. *Mary?* he says, and I smile. *Father,* I answer, the word catching in my throat. *I've been looking for you,* he says. He steps toward me, stops my hand as I unbutton my blouse, stares at my fat lip, my bruised neck. *Are you all right?* he asks, and I laugh. *Sure,* I say. *Here,* I guide his hand toward my waist, thinking he wants to strip me himself, but he tells me he just wants to talk to me, says he'll pay for the time. *I'm not up for a conversion right now,* I say, and he shakes his head and sits down on the bed. I sit beside him and he stares at me. *Priests have many jobs,* he says. *We lead people to healing waters, and those healing waters take many forms.* I nod. *Oh, Mary,* he says, *you are healing waters. Many a time I've remembered you and taken solace in that remembrance; you have been my salvation.* I wonder if he's drunk, if he's doing some sort of twelve-step program. *My congregation doesn't understand the dark soul that is the soul nonetheless, that drive that won't be calmed but by one thing, the need that unfilled can destroy you and the lives of those you love. But I do,* he says. *I understand.* His hands tremble as he fingers the gold cross around his neck, and I want to tell him to hide his gold and his cash, to think about what he's doing. *I've made you the dark savior, Mary,* he says, *and I'm sorry.* Here is a man in needless turmoil, I think, but I don't know how to say it. Business is business, don't sweat it? *Father,* I say, touching his drooped shoulder, and he asks if I understand the sanctity of the priestly confession. At first I think he's lost his mind, that he believes I am *the* Savior and as such can be his confessor. But then he mentions a man, a raucous yet fundamentally good man with a tattooed biceps, a troubled parishioner whose wife doesn't understand his earthly needs, his rage and humiliation after losing his job on the line when the tire plant shut down. *I've made you the unnameable savior of men,* he says, touching my hair gently, red strands flashing through his fingers, and then he stares at me for a long time, as if looking for a sign that I understand what he's done. *But now,* he says, *this man's gone missing, and it's my doing, all my doing. I've promised his wife I'd find him, and after I do I'll confess my sins. This is not your fault but mine. Do you understand the sanctity of the confession, Mary, that what you tell me I'll tell no living soul?* I think about John, feel certain he was breathing when I left him splayed across the belt, his head crowned in a halo of blood.

Nina's eyes grow large as the priest and I pass the front desk to exit the Serendipity, and we are silent as he steers his Town Car up Monroe toward Nathan, takes Nathan to Farley, Farley to the warehouse district. I've told him nothing, just asked him to take me for a drive. If John's car isn't there, I'll give the priest his wedding ring, tell him John said he loved his wife but wasn't good enough for her, that he's sorry for everything. Is it a sin, though, to pray that the rusted Monte Carlo is still parked sideways in the lot, its bumper kissing the chain-link fence, John's body resting peacefully on the line he once controlled? Is it a sin to envision that this would be the priest's inadvertent gift of dark salvation, a parallel deliverance for two people whose lives were plummeting, a cold and hard and violent plunge into eternally healing waters?

THINGS THAT NEVER COME

My wife makes up stories. She doesn't lie; she writes fiction, in which lying is not only legal but standard practice. That my wife doesn't lie outside her writing, though, hasn't helped our marriage.

"The sun has set on our time, Bobby," she says as she looks up, tracing an imaginary sun from its zenith on our stuccoed ceiling to its horizon on the badly scratched Pergo floor. Shelley tends toward the dramatic. It's New Year's Day, thirty-two below with the wind chill, the whole northeastern seaboard is shut down, and she's talking about the sun.

"Well," I say, not looking up from the *Times* I'm holding so tight it vibrates, "a rare snowfall in Mexico just killed millions of monarch butterflies, so there are worse things."

Don't get me wrong; the separation wasn't my idea and I still love my wife, but I'm reeling over how easy it is for her to leave me and then wax poetic about it. She's moving in short term with some guy from her writer's group I've secretly dubbed "Bluto."

You may think I'm naive, but I believe her when she says there's nothing going on between them. I've seen him.

A week after her sunset comment we argue about the credenza; I'm making her take it now so that maybe she'll contemplate the amount of work involved in leaving me. I carry the computer to her car, and I want to laugh when we slip and slide across the ice and almost drop what we're loading, but I don't. Shelley already thinks I'm immature. "Why do you sneak up on people?" she says. "Why do you laugh when someone falls? What are you, twelve?"

"Well, I guess that's it," she says as I jam her pillow into the backseat on top of the sari I'd bought her from Target—a gift, come to think of it, she never wore. "I'll be in touch."

She kisses me, deeply, then leaves me standing in the slush with a hard-on as she fishtails out of my life.

I trudge up the stairs and into the house, and the first thing I hear is the familiar click of Faulkner's nails across the wood floor—I get to keep Faulkner because Bluto is allergic to dogs. Faulkner's excited because he thinks this is Shelley's night out to the psychic or to the masseuse or to writer's group and he'll get to eat Bugles and watch the news with me on the sofa. What he doesn't yet know is that, from now until possibly eternity, he'll be able to do that every night.

I met Shelley in a geology class, where she often stared into space while the professor lectured. When I noticed the bells on her shoes, her Salvation Army coat, and her earrings, which were large plastic globes of the world, I wanted to save her. Actually, I was attracted to her not just because she was pretty and she had the confidence to wear that stuff, but because—and this seems like a terrible thing to admit—she seemed eccentric enough to turn off any competition. Shelley was tall and thin and cute, sure, but I learned that she was also as serious as an aneurysm. She aced tests without paying attention in class, haggled with waitresses over the meaning of "well done," and demanded and received free checking at our bank after catching a statement error that she was certain was part of a conspiracy to rob us blind. Then, after pulling sheets over the heads of life's daily crises, she'd stare at the teapot or the window ledge or the pencil in her hand for hours.

I learned through five years of marriage that her lost look meant she was directing fictional lives in some other dimension. "Check out that hawk!" I once said as we drove down Fifth Avenue in Manhattan, and she said, "I have to kill Maggie. I have no choice." All this as if we'd had dinner with this woman the night before.

"How are you going to do it?" I'd asked, just to appear interested.

"I don't know. How should I?"

"Hmm . . . parachute accident. Hannibal Lector. Run-in with a superhero." I mean, why not, when lying's not only legal but encouraged? Why not shoot the wad?

"What are you, twelve?" she said.

I guess my lack of interest in her writing got her thinking about our "incompatibilities." But that's not exactly right; I was interested in her writing. I guess I wasn't interested enough. I love her stories about the clown troupe that defects from the Russian circus while on tour in Egypt and the lunatic pool boy who kills his clients, and I told her so. The one about the couple who communicates without talking I just didn't get, and I told her that too. I was always honest, although I never said things like, "There is a Miltonian quality to the opening scene, like an invocation," or "The main character is somewhat nebulous; can you justify his pain?" These are the types of things members of her writer's group scrawled across copies of the stories I read. I just said things like, "This is a good story," or "Why can't these characters just *say* what they mean?"

A week after she moves out, Shelley calls to ask for a loan; Bluto's furnace had blown and since his house is so big he needs a big furnace to replace it. "Okay," I say, figuring that the money is at least one way to keep us connected. She picks up the check that day and hangs around to toss a tennis ball to Faulkner. She looks great; her hair is curled into little corkscrews, and I can tell by the sculpted curves under her leggings that she's been putting extra miles on the exercise bike.

"You look terrific," I say.

"So do you." She touches my face and her hands smell like toasted almonds. "I'm sorry, Bobby," she says. "I just need some time to figure this out."

"I understand," I say, although I don't.

When she leaves I'm suddenly grateful for this: I have a small house, an inexpensive furnace. "Winter," I say, "take your best shot."

In March I start fixing up the house, although my first job is to trim Faulkner's nails. He whimpers a little, but I calm him with assurances that our newly sanded and stained floor will be enticing to Shelley. I don't kid myself: I know it's the mention of her name and not aesthetic promise that comforts him. What comforts me is the hope that Shelley will fall in love with the renovated house, see my effort as setting a new precedent in thoughtfulness, and come home. I start in the kitchen, tearing out countertops and cabinets, ripping down paneling, and pulling up the indoor/outdoor carpet that Shelley hated.

There is wood—oak—under the greasy carpet, and I take this as a good sign. Or at least a money-saving one. I buy some varnish and a small sander and finish most of the floor in a couple of days. The corners I have to do by hand, but I just turn on the radio and lose myself in the work. *Switzerland was never neutral,* I think after the newscaster on WNYC says Swiss banks are holding money the Nazis stole from the Jews during the Holocaust, and as I yank out a piece of shoe molding, I suddenly feel as if Earth has fallen off its axis and that nothing—my life especially—will ever be right again. I feel sick and dizzy, frustrated and angry all at once, so I swallow it like I always do. But when the newscaster reports that some failed youth leader in Scotland killed sixteen first graders, I kick the open can of varnish across the room, splattering windows, walls, appliances. I'm really sorry now that I did it, but at the time not the threat of all-out war, or my imminent execution, or even the thought of Shelley's return could have stopped me.

It's several days before I go back into the kitchen, and by then I need a putty knife to scrape the dried varnish off the windows. Textured paint will cover the worm-shaped splotches on the walls, and if Shelley ever pays back the furnace loan, I'll just buy new appliances. In the meantime I pretend that Jackson Pollock has used my kitchen as a canvas. I've always liked Jackson Pollock. He was an active artist. He never simply stared into space.

When I finally tell the guys at work about our separation, Sam and Bernie take me to Tallie's for a few beers.

"Fuck her," says Sam.

"No," I say, "it's not like that. I want her back."

"In that case," he says, "I'm sorry."

We throw some darts, eat burgers dripping grease, and play George Thorogood on the jukebox. For the first time since Shelley left, my stomach isn't in knots. At about one in the morning some college kids enter and swarm the place. The boys sit along the bar downing shots of Jägermeister before commandeering the dart boards, while the girls thread their way around the pool tables jiggling to the macarena.

"Fellas," says Bernie. "It's time."

"That's what I like about you, Bernie," says Sam before turning to me. "You know when to quit."

By the end of March I have the kitchen painted and am growing accustomed to cooking chili on my speckled stove and putting dishes in my spotted dishwasher.

"That's real nice, Jackson," I say whenever I notice a new design emerging from the splatters like a Rorschach image. There is a disproportionate star on the dishwasher, a large number seven on the oven door, and a cockeyed arrow spans the top of the refrigerator. And even though I'm actually starting to enjoy my new abstract kitchen art, I know that this is something Shelley will never accept.

I was hoping to renovate one room each month, but at the beginning of April, when I tear out the old rust-stained toilet in our bathroom and see the wood rot beneath, I know my schedule's shot. Sam and Bernie come over to help me pull out the damp wood and put in a new subfloor, and then I install a shiny white aerodynamic Kohler with an oval tank and a chrome handle.

"Well, la-de-*da*," says Sam.

"It's a thing of beauty," says Bernie, wiping away a fake tear. "May I?"

Sure, I'm a little miffed that Bernie uses my new toilet before I do, and I feel oddly territorial, like Faulkner when Hoffet's Great Dane leaves a bundle on our front lawn. But in the grand scheme of things I tell myself it's no big deal. We crack a few beers and turn on the tube while waiting for the pizza, and suddenly Bernie starts choking as he points to the television.

"That son of a bitch," he yells, the beer gurgling in his throat. "That son of a *bitch*."

Staring at us with sunken eyes and disheveled hair, all scruff and attitude, grunge and bones is the deadliest bomber in U.S. history, Ted Kaczynski.

"Seventeen fucking years," says Bernie, shaking his head sadly, closing his eyes, accepting defeat. "Goddamn, Ted."

The news anchor says that after a seventeen-year manhunt, federal agents raided a remote Montana cabin and found the Unabomber right where they'd expected he'd be.

"Then why'd it take them seventeen years?" I ask.

"Because they're dumb fucks," says Bernie, who does not so much support the Unabomber as he detests federal agents, who had seized his father's property in Oregon a decade earlier after he'd refused to pay taxes. "How'd they get you, Ted?" he asks as if the unkempt lunatic is sitting across the room in the sallow flesh.

Sam stares at the TV, nose scrunched as if he smells something foul. "The guy's a wacko," he says, and Bernie just shakes his head.

The Unabomber makes me think of Shelley, and maybe this is a bad sign, although maybe it's no sign at all. Everything makes me think of Shelley now that she's gone. "There's a thin line between genius and insanity," she'd said after reading the Unabomber's antitechnology manifesto in the *Times* last fall, and my look must have had my disregard for him and his vigilante brand of justice written all over it. "His mind is amazing," she said. "Just the way he thinks. If I could capture that in a story—"

"But he's nuts," I said. "He *kills* people."

She stared at me for a long time and then spoke slowly, as if to a child. "I'm not justifying what he did, Bobby. I'm saying that the fact that *he's* rationalizing what he did is fascinating."

Shelley read the Unabomber's newspaper rant countless times: over breakfast, while pedaling the exercise bike, in grocery lines. She highlighted his justifications in yellow, his technical explanations in green, his passages of pure rage in orange. She said she wanted to "become" the Unabomber, to assume his worldview, to write from his perspective. I was relieved that she was never able to do it. But now, staring at him on the television screen, I wonder if the man who for so long was the object of my wife's attention will resume his role of obsessive importance in her life, will push me even further from her thoughts. I start to think that maybe if I do something desperate, something crazy, she'll regain interest in me. But when I consider scaling the Empire State Building, or piercing my nose, or slitting my wrists, I realize that I don't have the stomach for drama.

The next day I simply call her, and she says she's glad they caught the crazy son of a bitch, that she hopes he gets the chair. Maybe she's frustrated by her inability to become Kaczynski, or maybe she's just writing from a law enforcement perspective now. We make small talk for a while, and then she says she has to go, something about a reading at the bookstore. I hang up happy that she has ditched the Unabomber but disappointed in the conversation overall, and I start wondering about what I should have said, what magic words will make her want to come home. Then it hits me: her stories.

In the spare bedroom, the one Shelley used as an office, I fish through papers in the plastic milk crates until I find "Freedom in the Shadow of the Pyramid." I read it several times, trying to come up with some profound insight about it, about why I like the little midget clown Adolpho the best. He's the ringleader, the one who starts the whole defection business, a brave little guy, and then it occurs to me: irony. He's the leader but he's a midget. After reading a few more of Shelley's stories and thinking hard about why I like or don't like them, what's interesting or not interesting about them, I realize that I don't like picking stories apart. I just like reading them, being entertained by funny characters or learning new things that may or may not be true. So I decide to read them without thinking too much about the names of the characters or why a midget is a midget, and I get into them, really get into them, for the first time. Maybe that's because Shelley's not looking over my shoulder as I read, asking why I made the face I did, waiting like a collie in front of an empty food dish for my response. I want to call her and tell her how good these stories are, how much more I like them now that I don't feel pressured to like them, how talented she is. Even without dissecting her stories about a shrinking woman, a talking shark, or a group of Martians lost in a Wal-Mart, I can see that Shelley is a damn good story-teller.

Strange people, odd occurrences, drama and romance have always fascinated her. She somehow internalizes that stuff, makes it a part of her so she can spin it into something of her own. "I can use that," she said after hearing about a yogi in India who ate an entire car over the course of a year or reading that the king of hearts is the only king on playing cards without a mustache. She took the geology class to fulfill a lab credit but admitted she would have preferred taking "Life in Medieval England" or criminal psychology. So maybe I shouldn't have insisted we see *Ransom* instead of *Jane Eyre,* and I understand now that I should have bought her the collector's edition of *Wuthering Heights* instead of that sari for her last birthday. I could tell by her expression that she was disappointed.

"Sorry," I had said, staring at the scratched floor. "Get it?"

So I know exactly what to do when I see the front page article about the auction later this month—maybe some simulated pearls or a throw pillow, a brooch or a compact carved with Jackie's initials, something simultaneously romantic and odd. I call and they tell me I don't stand a chance, that the Sotheby's regulars are planning to cart the stuff out by the truckload. Would I like to order an auction catalog?

"Yes," I say. "That would be perfect."

I spend the next week cutting slabs of green and white ceramic tile to spec for the bathroom floor; I'm already off schedule, so I may as well get fancy with the tile cutter I'm renting at twenty bucks a day. I cut the tiles in half, in quarters, in eighths to create a semicircular mosaic on the floor that fans out from the base of our luminous toilet.

I'm grouting the bathroom tiles when the UPS man delivers it, and I stop midproject to wash my hands and change my clothes so I won't stain the fat, glossy hardback catalog for which I paid $90. The catalog is for Shelley, so I turn the pages gently, trying not to crease them. I later read in *USA Today* that a small tape measure sold for two thousand dollars, and an ugly little stool went for almost thirty-five grand. The cheapest item in the auction, a reproduction of an etching of Washington, D.C., valued at twenty bucks, sold for $2,070. How could I compete with that?

Sometime in the middle of May I set the final tile into the bathroom floor and that very day dismantle our poster bed so I can begin work on the bedroom. With any luck I'll have it finished by June 28, Shelley's birthday. I'll invite her to dinner, present her with the catalog, and then show her the house, something old, something new, proof that things can change. I run a rented cleaner over the stained peach carpet, but it still looks matted and soiled. As I contemplate tearing it up, Sam and Bernie stop by—they've been coming by every week after bowling since I told them Shelley left—to bug me about subbing on the league. The team's not doing well. I say I'll think about it, that I'm pretty busy with the house and all, and they always roll up their sleeves to pitch in. I ask them what they think of the carpet and they stare at it for a long time.

Finally Bernie says, "Up she comes."

The next night we kneel on the floor, sawing and clicking strips of wood into place while listening to talk radio. Manley Horscht discusses the huge asteroid that just whizzed past Earth, the national increase in strokes, the eight climbers who died on Everest, the preponderance of sluggish sperm, the morning after pill.

"Fellas," says Bernie. "We appear to be in a state of decline."

Sam, who is sweating profusely on the new wood slats, says, "So all this is for nothin'?" He sweeps his arm across the room, exposing a large half-moon stain on the armpit of his work shirt. "Why bother if we're gonna get blown to smithereens by an asteroid—"

"Or if we can't propagate the species long enough to enjoy that ex-*cep*-tional toilet?" says Bernie.

I don't tell them what I'm thinking—that Shelley will be back long before the next near miss with an asteroid or before I have a stroke or my sperm start misbehaving.

"Sam," I say, throwing him a kitchen towel, "wipe that up."

I finish the bedroom two weeks ahead of schedule—a new cherry wood floor, a double coat of canary on the walls, and some "snow-colored" pleated shades I bought on sale at Project Patio. Even though I don't like yellow nearly as much as Shelley does, I have to admit it looks nice. I spend the next week planting roses and daffodils—I'm pretty sure those are the flowers she put in one of her stories—and trimming trees and hedges.

Bluto answers when I call, covers the mouthpiece with his fleshy, gargantuan hand.

"Hey, Shel, it's for you," he yells, and I want to slam the phone into the crooked arrow. I mean, who is he to call her "Shel"?

"Hello?" she says.

In a split second I wonder if I should call her "Shel" to reclaim her or if that would be too obvious, too immature.

"Shelley," I say. "It's me."

"What's wrong?"

"Nothing's wrong. Faulkner's fine. I'm fine. I was wondering—I'd like to take you to dinner."

"Bobby—"

"For your birthday. Just for your birthday."

There is a long pause. "Okay, Bobby," she says. "Okay."

My palms are so sweaty the steering wheel is tacky, and I have to laugh at myself, how pathetic I feel driving to my wife's house in a suit I haven't worn since before we were married. Maybe Shelley wants me back and maybe she doesn't, I think; maybe I want her back because I don't know what else to want, because I don't know how to crawl into a new life and start over. Maybe I should be angry about it—the pain, the fear, the humiliation—and I guess I am, but confronting my anger now seems dangerous, so I slam it back into the shadows. When I pull up to Bluto's, she bursts through the front door, and I don't know if she's excited to see me or she wants to keep me from going inside. We are drinking red wine and eating calamari at Braddock's when I hand her the gift-wrapped catalog. I know I should wait until after dinner, or at least until after the greasy appetizer, but I can't. She wipes her fingers daintily and tucks a twisted strand of blonde hair behind her ear before smiling.

"I'll like it," she says, "no matter what it is."

Her comment, I know, is meant to be sweet, thoughtful, but

it hurts because I suddenly understand that it is a trained response to my gifts, to me in general, one calculated to dispel disappointment. She tears off the shiny gold wrapper after gently removing the four-dollar bow and stares for a long time into the heap of torn, crumpled paper.

"Thanks," she says, extracting the book from its bed of gift wrap. "Thanks a lot."

"It's the auction catalog from the Camelot collection. Jackie O."

"Ah," she says.

"I thought you could use it in a story. You know, the information."

"Oh, right," she says brightly. "Sure."

She holds the book for a long time, then places it on the seat next to her before launching into a superficial conversation about our jobs, our friends.

"How are Bernie and Sam?" she asks. "Still bowling?"

"Sure," I say, "but they're fighting like hell for last place."

"I never understood why you quit," she says. "They needed you."

I want to point out the irony of her comment, how this should not be lost on a person who spends so much time with thoughts and words. But I don't. Things are going all right. That's why I don't bring up her stories or tell her how talented I think she is. Why enter those stormy seas now?

"I have another surprise," I say, and as I watch Shelley tilt her thick mane in the dim candlelight, I am happy for the first time in months.

Even though it's dark when we pull up to the house, Shelley

notices the rose bushes the moment she steps from the car. She likes the slick dining room wood, the pattern in the bathroom tile, the new kitchen floor.

"What's this?" she asks, running her finger along the caramel-colored splotches on the stove. I know she's thinking I'm immature, that I made a mess I didn't bother to clean up, which is true but it isn't, and I know the wrong answer will corral all her negative thoughts about me into the present moment, will make her remember why she left in the first place.

"It's art," I smile, and she says, "Hmm."

"Here's the best part," I say, pulling her toward the bedroom. I consider telling her to close her eyes but decide that's too corny; the room should speak for itself. When she approaches the doorway, I flip on the light—actually a new dimmer switch—and decide against saying, "Ta-da!" Instead, I say nothing, and I avoid eye contact because I don't want to see the disappointment in her face.

She just says, "Bobby."

We make awkward love on the poster bed; I'm trying too hard and Shelley is reserved, or at least I imagine she's questioning herself every step of the way. The lights are on full tilt, beaming, shining, bouncing off the bright walls and casting my clumsy seduction into silhouette. When I ask if I can shut them off she looks hurt, so I tell her that she is very beautiful, that the walls are too bright, that I wanted to buy her a measuring tape for her birthday.

"What?" she says, and I go limp and slip out of her.

"I love you, Shelley. That's all. I want you to come home."

We disentangle ourselves and slide apart, then stare at the

ceiling, our big toes barely touching, neither of us pulling entirely away.

"Either you love someone or you don't," I say.

"I love you."

"Then come back."

She sighs. "I'm going away for a while, Bobby. I need to think."

"Haven't I left you alone? Given you time?"

She doesn't say anything, and I understand then that the trip is planned, the ticket bought, the deal done.

"With who?" I ask, even though I don't really want to know.

"No one, Bobby. Just me and my thoughts."

"When?"

"Next month. A few weeks, Bobby. Just a few weeks."

What can I do? At least all hope isn't lost. "Okay," I say, trying to poke my index finger vertically through one of her curls. "Okay. Happy birthday."

Faulkner and I drive Shelley to JFK, and we're all crying—Faulkner does this howling thing—as I yank her suitcases from the back of the Jeep. I want her to say that there is hope, that she has a good feeling about this, but she doesn't, and by the way we're all carrying on, I'd have to say that none of us has a good feeling about any of this. Although I know it's no use, I ask her again to stay, offer to pay for the airline ticket, and imagine burning it later after we make passionate love in our bright yellow bedroom. She kisses me, then disappears through the sliding glass doors. Even though we're parked illegally, Faulkner and I sit in the Jeep and wait until 8:02 when Flight 800 to Paris is scheduled for takeoff. We watch for the 747, the huge red-and-white tubular body, the large TWA logo on the tailfin; I just wave at every plane that takes off.

Windows unzipped, the wind crashing in from all sides, we leave the airport and head out the Belt Parkway and onto Rockaway Boulevard toward Prospect Park, a can of tennis balls and a six-pack cooler in the back. It's humid as hell, and Faulkner is panting hard, jumping from the back to the front seat. I know how he feels. We should be tired, drained, and I guess emotionally we are, but my mind is racing, my adrenaline pumping.

A breeze off the bay tempers the heat, and we make good time, probably because it's a Wednesday night. Within twenty minutes Faulkner is lapping up grounders like a pro. Nothing gets by him—pop flies, liners, curves—until he spots two black Labs fighting over an orange Frisbee, teeth hooked in, heads jerking wildly. He bounds toward them and leaps into the fray, trying to snap onto the Frisbee, but the Labs pull back, struggle away from him. He circles them several times, running frantically, barking and jumping, all hope, all trust, all desire, but the Labs continue to snarl and tug and spin away from him. He finally plops down on the grass and whines. I sit down beside him. I think about Shelley until I'm numb, until the thoughts stop jabbing into my gut, stop coming on like a shock. *She's gone,* I think. *Right now, this very minute, she's gone.* I put my arm around Faulkner, then I run my fingers through his thick yellow coat, smooth away the pain and the frustration and the disappointment, rub out the hope that makes us wait so patiently for things that never come.

THE STALWART SUPPORT OF THE OBSESSED

I knew a guy who lost his mind studying theory.

"I'm angry all the time," he said. "I want to hit people."

We were in graduate school, Bruce and I, both of us working on doctoral degrees in English lit. Of course we wanted to hit people: there would be no jobs for us on the far end, and we'd spent two years consuming literary theory, learning a language that would alienate us from the larger world once we left the gilded confines of PU. But in truth I say that only now, in retrospect. We didn't know these things back then, and, to be honest about how it all happened, I guess I have to go way back, back to when we were content, back to when we'd idolized the people who quietly dispensed insanity. During our first year in graduate school we immersed ourselves in this stuff, relished being knee-deep in mythocriticism and Foucault's notions of textual self-destruction, actually worked to replace our routine thinking patterns with the literary theory du jour.

"I can't find the remote."

"Who can?"

"Where'd you put it, man?"

"You can't *put* the remote anywhere. By virtue of being remote it's unattainable."

Looking back, we decimated many friendships by preaching the arbitrary nature of the linguistic sign. But we didn't care because we felt comfortably superior with this new tool in our holsters, this new lens through which we could view the inadequacy of language, could hold forth to our new roommate, a chemistry major, on the philosophical relevance of the impossibility of statement.

"Then why don't you just shut up?" he said. He moved in with two guys from the math department a week later.

He's just scared, we thought. Afraid to know his primary means of communication is flawed, unreliable, even oppressive. So we walked around with this secret weapon, this *bomb,* and people didn't even want to know, didn't want to know they were promoting a patriarchal, colonial discourse each time they opened their mouths.

"Score one for the DWEMs," we'd say when we heard words such as *mantel* or *history.* Everyone had it in for the Dead White European Males, the men whose seminal influence was the scourge of modern communication, so what was there to do but to jump in with both feet, to work at trampling any vestige of a discourse that privileged a specific demographic? Anger plus passion equals righteousness, and we were the living sum of that equation.

Our professors were our heroes and allies in what we came to view as an ignorant, primitive world. "The main effect of theory is the disputing of common sense," said our semiotics teacher. "Yep," we said. "Yep." We understood that the prevailing common sense was ludicrous, something that needed to be blasted out of existence and replaced. With what? We were working on that.

If we maligned the spoken word as wildly inadequate, we held the written code in ultimate contempt, considered it nothing more than an artificial and derivative representation of the spoken word, as our idol and icon Jacques Derrida would have us do. "It's a misleading sign of a sign," we told anyone who would listen. "We've even stopped writing papers for class. How can our teachers fail us when they are covertly espousing the denunciation of the written word?" Before long only the philosophy majors would listen to us and only then, I see now, to blow holes in our theories while allowing us to buy pitchers of beer.

"Signs should be as transparent as possible," Bruce argued that fateful night at the Bull Horn. "They should not get in the way, should not affect or infect the thought or truth they represent."

"Ha," said Lambert, the philosophy group's pseudo-Socrates. "You guys are too much."

"Well stated," I said sarcastically, though I wasn't sure if he was using simple language to underscore Bruce's point or to trivialize an argument we had spent days fortifying.

"You guys talk about a flawed language," said Socrates. "You say it's elastic and unreliable, say you crave transparency, and then you say things like, 'Folding and unfolding the roots of its slightest signs, the text explains itself.' I mean, what the hell is *that*?"

"It's the subversion of language," I said heartily.

They all laughed, and even Bruce shook his head weakly, the stitches that held together his mind perhaps unraveling even then.

"You're a philosophy major and you're talking to *me* about complex theoretical language?" I sniffed.

Socrates smiled savagely. "Believe me," he said, "I won't. But I'll say this: you guys are light-years behind us again. Philosophers have known for centuries that there is a problem with the thing and its name, that reality is inexpressible. Where've you *been?*"

"Playing clean-up, I guess," Bruce rallied. "Tackling the problem that's stymied you for two thousand years."

Socrates laughed an idiot's laugh, cackling and eternal in its own incendiary way. "It's an extinct exercise to us, a rhetorical problem we *created* and have long since dismissed," he said. "We're imperfect beings," he said as he pointed his beer mug at me. "How can we create a perfect language?"

"We're not seeking perfection," I said. "We're simply seeking a better language."

"What's *better?*" asked the bartender, and I wasn't sure if he was mimicking the inane philosopher's never-ending rhetorical question or defending our argument concerning the unreliability of language.

"Right there," said Bruce, stabbing the air as if shooting the bartender twice with his index finger. "Right there. What's *better?* What's *truth?* What's *beauty?* God," he exhaled through his teeth. "Geez."

The philosophers stopped smiling and shook their heads in

tandem, as if they'd practiced for this moment. "Old news, boys," said Socrates. "Old news."

"Oh, forget words," said Lennie, playing Socrates' Plato. "Let's talk about punctuation. Who's the guy come unhinged over the quotation mark—I'm sorry, the *double mark?*" The philosophers all laughed as if at an inside joke, but weren't we accustomed to that?

"Derrida, of course," I said. "He's got a valid point. Why should the word enclosed—no, *trapped*—between the quotation marks be imprisoned when it is no less guilty of fraud than any other word? If you read *Dissemination*—"

"Right," said Plato. "All I see is a guy attacking his own tools with his own tools. He uses punctuation to tell us how faulty punctuation is, then he wails about it. What other discipline *does* that, spends all its energy cannibalizing itself? Have you guys run out of novels or something?"

"We've just found a better lens through which to view them. And Derrida's not wailing," I said. "An intelligent person could see that." Plato rose from his stool—philosophers, it seems, will defend their flimsy perspective at all cost—but he was a philosopher, after all, acne scarred and whiny, so I continued my defense. "He's simply showing by example the dire need for a more *exact* system of communication."

"Then why doesn't he spend his time creating one instead of bitching about the one he has, the one he's used to dupe slavish English majors into lionizing him?"

Plato leaned forward, the bulk of him aimed at me. *Pathetic* is the nearest word I can muster to describe it.

"He's a manipulative bastard, if you ask me," he went on. "They all are." He gulped down the remainder of his beer, the beer for which I had paid, and stared at me, his eyes wavy behind thick lenses.

"Well, I *didn't* ask you," I said. "What's more, I think *you're* a manipulative bastard. I'm not cowed by your grandstanding. I'm not cowed by your denial strategies. Go ahead and act tough to mask your fear, your refusal to confront a problem that threatens to expose your deep inadequacies."

The bar grew quiet. For someone else the silence might have been intimidating, but I'd built my reputation on a soapbox in a bar grown still. Plato continued to stare, vacantly it seemed, his eyes swimming under glass, and I launched into verbal castration.

"Clearly we're dealing with two different perspectives that by their very nature—one being right and one being *wrong*—won't yield a synthesis," I said. "Clearly Mr. Derrida speaks a language you can't hope to understand. Clearly you're a lemming who unwittingly contributes to an insidious system of confusion and oppression." I poked my finger into his pimpled face, laughed the laugh of the victor, and that's when he broke my nose.

"People are intimidated by theory," I said as Bruce steered his beat-up Pacer toward County General.

"Fight the good fight, my friend," Bruce said softly, blinking at the windshield, looking utterly lost.

Later that night, less than two hours after I'd shed blood for the cause, Bruce says he's losing his mind.

"I'm losing the line between the signifier and the signified," he said. "I can't achieve a solid cognitive structure."

I admit it: I was jealous. I mean, this was something, right? In a world where only the hyperintelligent realize there is no true solid cognitive structure, Bruce was *experiencing* it. Who knew where this strategy could take him, what new and brilliant literary theories this event could hatch?

"You've *got* to submit a new dissertation proposal," I said, suppressing my envy for the greater cause.

He shook his head. There were tears in his eyes. "I'm losing my *mind*," he whispered. He said he felt the two halves of his brain coming apart and rejoining in odd shapes: cups, tubes, parallelograms whose sharp edges poked the inside of his head; he said he could see a new language unfolding in his brain like the definitive strands of DNA.

"You're on to something," I said. "You are *on* to something."

He filled the Looney Tunes notebooks I bought on sale at Buy Rite, scribbling vigorously for hours on end. His notes made little sense to me, but I had yet to make the intellectual/theoretical leap he had. I could only read his journal and shake my head in awe:

> *The idea is younger than itself at a time when, in becoming older, it coincides with the present. But the present is with the one always throughout its existence. Therefore, at all times the idea both is and is becoming older and younger than itself, which means that a form that is one and the same will be at the same time, as a whole, in a number of things that are separate and consequently will be separate from itself. In that sense, it consistently fails at meaning anything.*

Bruce was doing just what our beloved theorist Roland Barthes would have us all do: peeling back the layers, tearing down the text, destroying the illusion of meaning. In short, deconstructing. It did not look easy. I brought Bruce chili and sunflower seeds, coffee and sardines. He stopped leaving the dorm; he stopped bathing; he stopped talking, channeling all his time and energy into the journal. Most of the time he was on fire, so fevered that I imagined I saw steam rising from his scalp, a halo of mist and fury. I don't want to overstate it, so I won't.

When our "Cixous and the Problem of Pronouns" teacher inquired about Bruce, I took her aside conspiratorially and told her about the breakthrough. "He's changing the dissertation," I said, "to 'Cognitive [Dys]Function: The Reflection of a Transitional Mind from within a Transitional Mind.'"

She stared at me. She squinted. She said, "I want to talk to him."

I smiled: she would love this. "He's way past all that. He's broken the fetters that bind him to that—to *this!*—toxic code of communication."

"Well, what code is he using to *write,* then?"

A trick question, to be sure, but not a very clever one when posed to a person trained in the art of the new L=A=N=G=U=A=G=E. "He has subverted the code out of existence," I smiled.

"Get him in here," she snapped.

But Bruce would not go to Dr. Sheckles, which is not surprising when you consider that he would not even go to the shower. She did not understand that Bruce himself was the antilanguage, that there was no longer a demarcation between him and his philosophy, that he had, ipso facto, *become* theory. Many celebrated theorists were attempting just that, but I doubt any were doing it

with Bruce's success. He had made his mind the field of decon-
struction, the crucible for language, the medium for all we had
dreamed of producing, and when I watched him work, I knew
it could be done. He drew faith from me like a magnet; I knew
that he would blast the old code out of existence, would usher us
into a new mind-set and prepare us for a paradigm shift that I
couldn't begin to fathom. Bruce, like theory, was a body in flux.
How could he go to Dr. Sheckles?

"Then I'll go to him," she offered.

"That's impossible," I said. "I can deliver a message. I can
bring you his response," though admittedly my ignorance pre-
cluded me from understanding, at least directly, most of his re-
sponses.

"I want to see *him*."

"You can't," I argued.

"Why not?" She leered at me suspiciously.

"Because the original is always deferred, you know that. He's
gone. Bruce *has* left the building." I had no idea of the prophecy
of those words; I had no idea that Bruce's shifting mental construction was at that moment tripping a psychic implosion.

"Ah," said Dr. Sheckles, who told me to tell Bruce to drop his
classes. "Stop covering for him," she said. "Especially if he's not
even here."

So I was alone and in charge of a genius, if anyone can say
that he is in charge of anything. It was up to me to channel this
wellspring of literary brilliance to a community whose own repre-
sentatives were too shortsighted to grasp it. Bruce's parents were,
fortunately, on a ten-and-a-half-week tour of the world's pinot
noir vineyards, and his brother was serving out a three-month

term in the Boston Youth Authority for breaking four upper-floor windows in the homes of each member of the Clack County Board of Education. They were, in hindsight, a precise, obsessive family.

Bruce lost weight, and sometimes he cried while scrawling notes across the paper, ignoring margins, often scratching long after his pen had run out of ink. This was the only thing that upset me: the loss! So I made sure he had a jar of Bics at his disposal, and I put food on separate plates—nothing could touch in his formalist phase—turkey slices, cherry tomatoes, potato chips, in the hope that he would regain some weight before his parents returned and his brother had served out his sentence. Surely they would take him away: How could I expect them to understand, to sublimate their fear to the gifts for which Bruce now labored, gifts that by virtue of their brilliance we may never fully comprehend? After all, most complex ideas can be apprehended only after reflection, perhaps years and years and years of reflection. It was a leap of faith, I tell you, but there was an instinct you didn't question, and that instinct was theory incarnate, and that theory incarnate was Bruce.

Two months after Bruce stopped attending classes, the university sent letters to him at the dorm, copies of which probably were collecting dust in his parents' foyer beneath the mail slot. He opened them, turned them over, and immediately began to scrawl crosswise on the backs. Later I read the neatly typed threats on the letterhead side: probation, failure, suspension. As if anyone at the university were qualified to qualify Bruce! Albert Einstein and John Lennon were bad students—need I say more? A little longer, that was all. Bruce seemed to be approaching something, slowing a little, arriving. His most recent entry indicated this to me as closely as anything he had ever written had indicated anything to me:

> *Relevance! A shifting social construct no one thing of course never just one thing that must be done and redone continually to arrive at meaning, true meaning, inherent meaning exposed truth (and antitruth disguised but not disguised as reverse truth) the thing we all know but can't say I will say I will say I am! (Almost)*

Would I have done things differently had I known that Bruce's mother was likely being thwarted from counting each grape on each vine by her husband, a man destined to spend his life pulling her away from light switches and door locks (the binary nightmares of the obsessed), a man who himself would become obsessed with her cure? What if I'd known he had ferried her from one analyst trained in obsessive-compulsive disorders to the next in reverse alphabetical order so that he could help to demarginalize the letters X, Y, and Z? It's hard to tell. My disdain for the prevailing language ran so deep that at times I felt something akin to despair, and this desperation fueled my hope in an apt reward for the just: I was poised to miss the signs. *Why not Bruce?* I thought. He'd worked as hard as any of us to burn down the system of codified inequality and institutionalized confusion while constructing a feasible replacement. Why not?

I was a disciple, pure and simple, and my conversion would not have been complete without my own gift of insight, with which I was struck two days before his parents stormed the dormitory and shuttled Bruce off to the Mayo Clinic and three days before Dr. Sheckles was fired for publishing portions of "Cognitive [Dys]Function: The Reflection of a Transitional Mind from within a Transitional Mind" in the campus literary journal *Logos* (was it my responsibility to know that she was already on probation for plagiarizing an article that had appeared in *Echo, Echo, Echo* when I slipped a notebook into her mailbox?). My insight was sudden. There had been hints, to be sure, but on that most memorable night I started to fully comprehend Bruce's writings, to decode what before had looked to me to be only gibberish. His text had cracked open my mind and I began to know what it must feel like to be Bruce. I admit it: I was no longer jealous. Negotiating his unconventional syntax, decoding his notes, and placing his free-form art into context was a practice in unobstructed interpretation. Not for a moment did I doubt my insights were correct. Bruce *had* created a system of communication so precise that he'd ferried me, for brief snatches anyway, into the psychic realm. He'd created something—a precise metadiscourse, the Esperanto of literary theory, a mind meld—but how to apprehend it in more than fleeting moments, how to view it in larger than hairline cracks in cognition? *That* was the challenge.

"Bruce," I shook him awake after comprehending four consecutive pages of scrawl. "I get it," I said. "You can talk to me in your language. Can you speak it, or is it exclusively written?"

"Of course," I cried. "You've inverted the order of creation!" Momentarily I thought of speaking backward to him, but that would have been ridiculous. My desperation frightened me, as did the feeling that I was riding the edge of a new paradigm and that if I veered any further I could easily become the dirty, emaciated person I saw before me. Were I to follow him into the uncharted territory of the postpostmodern theoretical mind, could I ever regain admittance to my former one? Would I wish to?

"My God," I said. "Talk to me, Bruce. I need to know what's going on in there. Should I follow you in?"

Bruce stared at me, stonefaced.

"I understand," I cried. "I can see it—in glimpses, anyway. It's difficult and frightening, to know and to not know. I can't seem to hold on to it unless I let go of everything else."

Bruce stared at me, stonefaced.

"Let me see the books," I said. "I can decipher your theory. I can make you famous."

He pulled the books closer to his chest; he laughed until there were tears in his eyes.

"Talk to me, Bruce. I can understand you now."

But, of course, Bruce couldn't share his insights. Perhaps he had devised a better code, but how could he explain it with the substandard language at his disposal? He was too far removed from the old language to do the translation anyway, so it would be up to me, the person riding the edge of both codes, to articulate my psychic apprehension of the text, even if that required poring over it ceaselessly for those minuscule moments of insight. I owed that much to Bruce for his struggle.

"Give me the books," I pleaded. "I can do this."

Bruce then spoke for the first time in two months. "I'm angry all the time. I want to hit people," he whispered. "I want to hit *you*."

That made sense. Or it had started to make sense, but I wasn't ready to welcome him back into the world of lesser logic, into my world, not when we were so close.

"Let's talk about the work," I begged. "Let's talk about the newest language."

He bowed his head and rested his chin atop the pile of note-books on his chest. "I," he whispered. He coughed a racking cough, as if blowing the dust out of his stagnant vocal chords, and said, "I question this."

"No," I said softly, and I reached over to touch his bony shoulder, something I realized only then that I had not done in a long time. "What you've done, whatever that is, is important. It will make a difference to someone, someday, I'm sure of it. It's all right to question; the work will stand up to that. Questioning is good."

He squinted at me through strands of greasy hair. He said, "I question your sanity."

His look was simultaneously pathetic and hateful, and for the first time I questioned the price of his insight, the value of the prize. Certainly Bruce himself would give anything—his life, even—to accurately codify thoughts and concepts, to launch an egalitarian and precise universal language that would pave the road to social, political, and gender equity. But what good is the language if no one else comprehends it?

I slumped down onto the futon next to him and stared at the array of food-encrusted plates on the coffee table before me; I let go and the moment passed, my protocognition already a shadow of a shadow. Confusion assailed me as never before, and as I stared at a desiccated hump of apple skin fused to a paper plate, I wanted to cry.

Bruce then sat upright and began counting the notebooks before flinging them across the room. There were sixty-four in all. "Excess violates proportion and makes for bad art and bad ethics," he croaked.

Just when I thought it couldn't get worse, he became a philosopher.

"There is no excess when you're creating new *theory,* Bruce."

"Theory is endless," he said. "Anything that is endless is by its very nature excessive."

He had a point. In fact, his proclamation of theory as excessive comprised the penultimate line in his final notebook. The last line simply said "Cheese."

We sat side by side on the futon for several hours, silent, haunted, and that's when I caught up to Bruce. That's when I saw what Bruce saw, and I saw that he saw that I saw what he did. Subversive energies coursed through me; I wanted to break plates, smash windows, burn the stacks of notebooks scattered about the room. Why? Because I had glimpsed the final truth, one that Bruce had labored against daily: that nothing exists if we can't name it, that there would never be consensus, that constructing a new and better language was as impossible as negotiating the existing one. Our objective would require the world to end and begin again. From scratch. All over. We could never create something new with the existing materials. I felt certain there must be numerous scientific theories to prove it. Bruce had become the microcosm of the linguistic apocalypse; exorcism of the old code had proved impossible, the effort instead triggering self-destruction.

Pathetically, I labored against it for only three hours; I threw up the theoretical white flag; I trafficked in clichés left and right when I called his parents: over the top, off the deep end. Then I walked around the dorm room, trying to collect the pieces of my mind that I'd thrown off during the past two months: reason, temperance, things like that. Bruce had spread the notebooks evenly across the floor and then proceeded to fall asleep on them, diagonally, his fist in his mouth. Did I still think he was a genius? Yes, insofar as anyone who has stepped over the edge of conventional logic and looked into the eye of the abyss can be. But when I allowed Socrates to glean the notebooks after Bruce had been carted off in his mother's spotless Rolls Royce Silver Spur and he accused Bruce of sophistry, I couldn't construct an argument. Was I tired? Did I agree? I can't say because that moment is gone and I can't or won't remember. Over beers for which they had paid the philosophers accused Bruce of doing the very thing that the greatest literary theorists railed against but were themselves guilty of— fabricating the things they claimed already existed in the work: strategies, perspectives, authorial intent. Those things grew out of the investigation rather than out of the text. Their findings were, in a word, contrived. For what? Grants, tenure, adoration, who knows? Were they geniuses or mercenaries? Frankly, I no longer cared to think about it, though for a time the philosophers tried to kick-start my interest, tried to place me back on speaking terms with passion.

"Listen, the great artist is one who does not misrepresent the world but who discloses its real nature," said Socrates, "and in this way Bruce will always be a great artist. He was truly *human.*"

I imagine he saw Bruce as someone who followed his passion well past the end zone, who taxed the limits of psychic endurance as only a driven yet fallible being can. But to me Bruce had only disclosed the real nature of literary theorists: focused, determined, self-sacrificing, yes, but also arrogant, insular, self-confirming. Of course, I did not believe all these things immediately, though the vision of Bruce shuffling across the commons, buttressed by his perfectly coifed parents, twisted something inside me, something that I would spend a long time untwisting. They were a trio of intent, moving rhythmically away from me, swaying in tandem toward a grail of prescription pills and mental therapy. But I didn't know that then, nor did I know that Bruce would later be diagnosed with hypergraphia, a mental condition whose sufferers battle their frustrated efforts at communication by compulsive writing, scribbling, and drawing. I simply believed that Bruce was a noble soul who had sacrificed himself to the purification of language—something that I suspected, as I surveyed the dog-eared notebooks, I was too small to do. I surrendered that day, slowly and unconsciously, while watching Bruce's form recede into the pane of the sun-blasted window. As I stared at him, trapped between the perfect parentheses that were his parents, the sash of his robe fluttering behind him like a useless rudder, I allowed myself to wonder how I could have put all my hope into something so frail, something so fragile, something that would fall apart without the stalwart support of the obsessed.

So I say, "Let it slam, blow it out, rip the roof off," and he just stares at me.

"I can't do this," he says, hands up as if I'm pointing a gun at his perfectly square jaw, his Tommy Hilfiger T-shirt, his blond highlights, the speck of coke clinging to the reddened edge of his left nostril.

"All I'm saying is you gotta *kill* somebody in a thing like this."

"Didn't Stu tell you I'm doing this different? Didn't Stu tell you I had a vision?"

"Well, from where I sit it ain't 20/20."

"And from where I sit you're done, and Stu's done too. Dumb fuck."

"Que será será," I say, he goes ballistic with the patio furniture, and suddenly two guys the size of minivans are helping me to my Caprice.

"Watch the shirt," I say as they yank me by the arms across a manicured lawn the size of Dodger Stadium, "it's my only Armani."

With that they pull harder, and I drag behind and stare at the back of their heads—I won't make this easy 'cause it's not in my nature to make things easy—and I see that they have no necks. Well, I suppose that can be useful.

The kid I won't bother to name because he's just another rich moron with enough money to catapult a ridiculous idea onto a movie screen. The vision, the *cutting-edge* script he wants me to write: a murder mystery without a murder.

"Get it?" he asked when we first met at Spago, bourbon-marinated prime rib and Dom P. on him. Or on his father. Same mansion. Same credit card. Same stupid grin.

"No," I said, shoveling it down before we reached the stalemate I knew from experience was coming.

"It's a kinder, gentler murder mystery."

My first instinct was to ask if he'd just said "kinder, gentler," but the beef was like butter and my mind was rocking in the arms of $500-a-bottle alcohol. "Go on."

"It's like the mystery that is solved is there is no mystery. We got some evidence to the contrary—maybe grape juice in the car and trunk, some severed fingers it turns out were from a factory accident, but we got no actual murder. Just everyone thinks there was, and they get all scared and shit, and the hard-ass detective—I see Johnny Depp here—is busting down doors, but at the end— and this is the sweet spot, Bob, this is the prize: the final shot is the camera following the single tear trickling down Johnny's face before it lands on the butt of his gun because he's so happy, so fucking elated no one's dead. People will be crying, man, they'll just be losing it."

My look must have indicated something, because he continued his excruciating analysis: "They come to the theater expecting death—we'll have to finesse the PR big time but I know a guy—and instead they get life. They leave freakin' ecstatic that nobody bought it." He has that heady look of triumph and certainty, a look only a kid who's been told all his life he's better than he really is can have.

"How old are you?" is what I wanted to say. What I said was, "This is unprecedented."

"Precisely." He smiled, his coke-shot brain misinterpreting my comment.

"I don't know if we can make that work. Maybe we can write it as a comedy."

"Dude," he said, "Bobby, my man. Don't worry, I got it all up here."

He tapped his beautiful blond head and I thought I saw dead brain cells exploding from his ears. I knew then that he wouldn't be dissuaded, but I let him invite me to the mansion the next day anyway, refused to feel guilty as I sat poolside on a chaise lounge that probably cost more than my monthly earnings. After downing four Hurricanes and a platter of crustaceans large enough to fill a tide pool, I explained that after serious consideration I'd concluded that a murder is an integral part of a murder mystery, no two ways. Ironically, he grew violent, tossing lawn furniture into the pool and trying to spear me with the sharp end of a tiki torch. And then the minivans were upon me.

As I smoothed a crease on the left shoulder of my sky-blue Armani and stared at a dot I hoped to hell wasn't a hole, I wondered what I'd tell Dana, the woman of my dreams about a quarter of the time. When I first met Dana, she admired what she saw as my integrity.

"I just can't do it," I'd explained to her after some woman from San Diego asked me to doctor an X-rated script featuring talking insects, something about *Playboy*-meets-Kafka.

"It's your artistic sensibility," she'd said, and I didn't contradict her, though it wouldn't be long before she would contradict herself. The fact is, I can't write a script with talking animals because animals don't talk, and I can't write a murder mystery in which there isn't a murder. Call it lack of vision, which these days I'd take as a compliment.

But it wasn't long before Dana started holding Visa bills and mortgage coupons under my nose and saying things like "Maybe there actually is a parallel universe" and "Just because a person's never sprouted wings before doesn't mean it can't happen." Now she says she doesn't care if I write about Vikings plundering a Wal-Mart or the cast of *South Park* piloting a rocket to Alpha Centauri, as long as it brings in cash. We've lived together for three years. People change.

I'm still wondering about the dot on the Armani when I pull up to the house. Luke is in front of the TV watching cartoons, a two-liter Coke bottle wedged between his legs. His eyes are red and puffy; he's been sleepwalking again.

"Where's your mom?" I ask.

He shrugs. "Diner?"

Dana is a waitress at Sal's. That's where we met shortly after

I awed critics with the lines I'd penned for *The Asylum,* shortly after I'd plunked two grand onto the counter at Village Jag for the hunter-green model with the tan leather seats. I fell into something when I first saw Dana, and I still fall into it every once in a while when the moon is just right and the volume on life is turned down low. When she slammed the club sandwich onto the counter and looked at my face, I thought I would say what I was thinking: *I want to nail you. Hard.* But she already knew it, and later that night she let me. I still eat at Sal's when I run out of desperate people with no talent but enough money to take me to Cicada or Drago and try to convince me to write a script with a thousand characters or a script with no characters or a murder mystery with no murder.

"Hey, bud," I say to Luke. "What time she leave?"

He shrugs again, his eyes fixed on the television, SpongeBob the Svengali of his six-year-old brain. She probably shouldn't leave the kid alone, but I can't say anything, especially now that it's officially my fault she's back at Sal's, according to her. According to me, I'm not his father.

Just as I'm thinking about that, Dana flies through the front door—Dana never enters a room but rather bursts on the scene—and rushes to Luke as if he's on fire. "What did I tell you?" she cries, then looks at me as if I'd been standing here watching him burn. She snatches the bottle of Coke from between his legs and he lets out a small cry. Luke has been diagnosed with diabetes, but don't diabetics need sugar too? Aren't they the ones who go into comas without it? The day they returned from the doctor, she red-eyed and he slapping together a pair of plastic hands he'd lifted from the toy bin at the pediatrician's, she'd said, "It's not a death sentence." This has become the mantra at 124 Alley Road, the small house resounding with the refrain, the words crawling up and sliding down the yellow plaster walls. "Hey, Ma," Luke says as she pokes his tiny arm with the needle, "it's not a death sentence." Dana slices an apple into a bowl of yogurt and says, "It's not a death sentence," as if the only thing worse than shots and yogurt is death.

"I brought you something to eat," she says to Luke and snaps open a Styrofoam container with a geriatric lunch: a lump of cottage cheese and peaches and a carton of skim milk. Overnight he's gone from six to sixty, but I won't say it. Not now. The way Luke gazes at the food, runs his finger along the sharp edge of the box, I can see he's given up. When Dana tells him to eat, he moves the spoon mechanically from the gelatinous mass to his lips. Then she turns to me.

"So how'd it go with the rich kid?" she says. "The murder mystery."

"His vision defied my artistic sensibility."

"Yeah?" she says. "Well, right now we can't afford your artistic sensibility."

We live in a shit hole on Alley Road in Culver City, trapped in the shadow Hollywood throws across the rest of the country, hell, the rest of the world. I guess that says it all about the state of my screenwriting career. One day you're on—John Irving is returning your calls, Geena Davis is winking at you on the set, Spielberg is asking how you feel about Michener's epics—and the next day you're placed on hold, told by the security guard at MGM that he doesn't want any trouble. Is it because of your artistic sensibility? Is it because the twentysomethings who can't write a complete sentence but whose fathers run the industry have blacklisted you? Is it because the public palate is so radically altered that people who once demanded refunds at the box office now sit glassy-eyed and broken before the big screen? Who in the hell knows. All I know is that I've collaborated on some damn fine scripts—you may have heard of a little film called *American Beauty* or seen the multimillion-dollar movie *Forrest Gump*—and I've not changed the way *I* do things.

Stu, my agent, says the business is fickle, that I just need another great story to launch me back to the top. Then he sets up meetings with kids who want to rewrite *Lord of the Rings* as a musical. Stu latched on to me right after *Twilight*, my adaptation of Stephen King's umpteenth novel, and he rode the waves of *Near* and *Milan,* both script-doctoring gigs he'd gotten from the kids of his director pals who knew they weren't worth the ink and paper it took to print them. But *Near* and *Milan* were more than doctoring; they were the amputation and angioplasty of revision. Under my scalpel those stories blew the top off the charts. Both were nominated for Oscars, and the papers said I "was robbed by a *Titanic* mistake in 1997" and that in 1998 "the great Elizabethan author himself would call it a tragedy that *Shakespeare in Love* stole the Oscar from *Milan.*" Not my words. But now these kids have *vision.* Now you can't alter their scripts. They all want to be the next Sofia Coppola. "I want to write the antiscript," they say, "I want to write the story of my life." This one's draped across a patio chair at La Cachette in a three-piece suit and Birkenstocks, drinking hundred-year-old wine that is eighty years older than he is and eating caviar with his fingers. "It's hell," he says, "my life is pure hell. You don't even know."

"Even Winston Churchill and the Dalai Lama didn't write their stories until they were well into their fifties," I say.

"Who?" he says.

"Listen, can I take some liberties with the character?" I ask. "Add some juice?"

"Believe me," he snorts as he throws his platinum AMEX card on the table, "you won't need to. It's all me."

At times like this I miss Omar. Omar was my first agent. Omar would never have entertained this kid. Omar was sensible, except for when he landed me the Stephen King script by telling the director I was a savant.

"Omar," I'd said, "do you know what a savant is?"

"Yes," he'd said, "you. From here on in you're a savant."

Actually, I don't think MGM cared if I was a savant or not. They'd already hired and fired nine screenwriters and burned nine scripts. King didn't care—he'd already gotten most of his—and the studio seemed neutral, but the director was a ball breaker. You've heard of him, and since he threatened to sue me the last time I got drunk and wrapped my arms around his knees, I'll just leave it at that. The bottom line is this: The director was desperate. The guy loved Omar, and Omar loved me, and I now think that Omar really thought I was a savant. His belief in me is what wrote that script; his belief in me had the ball-breaking director whistling on the set and Stephen King sending me a case of Chivas and a leather-bound copy of his latest novel, one of which I really enjoyed. When Omar fell asleep at the wheel of his Bentley Arnage convertible and sailed from the Pacific Coast Highway into San Luis Obispo Bay, I got drunk and sought out the aforementioned director at Mastro's to toast the life of our mutual friend. That was the first of several times the sky-blue arms of my Armani were wrapped around his legs. Liquor is my enemy.

I think my scriptwriting career died with Omar. Sure, I did all right with *Near* and *Milan,* but something was slipping even then, and it wasn't me. It was the times, the demands, the new writers. They wrote stories, the same stories they'd written before, the same stories other writers had written before. I don't mean in an archetypal way: the good guys win the war or the boy gets the girl. I mean the *same* stories. Take *Finding Forrester.* Didn't I see that same movie starring Robin Williams and Matt Damon when it was called *Good Will Hunting?* Isn't *My Big Fat Greek Wedding* the retarded first cousin of *Moonstruck?* What's the difference between *The Manchurian Candidate* and *Rambo* besides location and face paint? Now we have *Herbie: Fully Loaded, Bewitched, War of the Worlds, Oceans Eleven, Charlie and the* frickin' *Chocolate Factory.* I don't want to rewrite the same stories even if those are the only ones Hollywood will produce in a bloodsucking effort to wring all the profits it can out of one idea, to beat it until it's brain dead, to drive in the risk-free zone. Stu hasn't sold one of my original scripts in four years. Four years. I've tried to write a novel, but I'll tell you this: I don't have the temperament.

Dana used to say I had the temperament to do anything I set my mind to because I was smart. Now she says I must not want to do anything, wondering aloud how hard could it be to convince a coke addict that my idea is his or to write the retarded *second* cousin of *Moonstruck.* The problem is that she met the nitwits whose mentally challenged brainchildren, originally called *Breath on My Neck* and *Under a Dark Red and Sometimes Blue-green Italian Sky,* turned into *Near* and *Milan* under my firm and aggressive scalpel. These guys were the quintessential Dumb and Dumber, but after the Oscar nominations they became dangerous in their conviction that *they* had actually conceived the brilliant subplots and character arcs and that they could do it again. Dana mistook stupid for charming, a mistake she has not outgrown.

"Why can't they write their own stories?" she asked right after Dumb was arrested for bludgeoning his valet with a croquet mallet.

"They don't write sentences," I said. "They serve them."

Dana is a beautiful woman, though she was never more beautiful than when she swung her legs from the Jag, lifting a firm ass wrapped in red silk Gucci from the leather seat and catwalking into Madeo like she owned the place. She was sexy when she mispronounced *Bordeaux,* when she fluttered her false eyelashes at me over oysters Rockefeller, when the glitter she'd dabbed on her face and neck winked in the candlelight. There's an element of trashy to Dana—and I'm not complaining, believe me—that was trimmed down to perfection when we were dining off Hollywood's gravy train. She'd shelved the halter tops and the raccoon eyes, the electrified hair and the six-inch heels. It was as if she was less desperate somehow, less eager to provoke men's stares, calmer in her more moderate self, and this was, in a word, hot. We rented a townhouse in the Hollywood Hills for a while, had sex in the Jacuzzi, on the balcony, hell, even in bed. We couldn't get enough of each other. But during that time we also learned a sad truth:

that money makes people beautiful or crazy, sometimes both and seldom simultaneously. We had a chance to be beautiful, but the train pulled into a station and dumped us off long before the crazy stop. This is what I try to tell Dana, that selling the Jag and moving to Culver City isn't a bad thing, that we have a chance to work for it all over again. She says she doesn't mind working, it's not that, but she wants a better life for her son, who's had a tough go so far.

Luke was three when I met Dana, but his personality was already set. Neither he nor Dana knew Luke's father very well, an aspiring actor who'd waited one too many tables and attended one too many ill-fated casting calls before he threw himself off a granite cliff near Overlook Trail on the Pacific Coast Highway. His body was never found, but the eyewitness accounts of several bicyclists who tried in vain to lure him from the edge have satisfied anybody who cared enough to ask. According to Dana, one of the cyclists pretended to remember his stunning performance in *All the Way to Jupiter,* a B-rated sci-fi flick in which he had a walk-on role, but he only smiled, waved once, and jumped. Liquor was his enemy too. Sometimes I imagine him and Omar floating over the Pacific in the Bentley, talking about what a crapshoot this business is, weighing their successes and failures through each other's eyes. Once I imagined this guy jumping right into Omar's ghost cruiser as it sailed the jagged cliffs up and down the coast, and neither of them was surprised. Maybe Omar said, "What took you so long?" and the guy just shook his head and said, "Slow learner." I've even dreamed that Omar asked me this very question, though I woke up before I could answer.

This loose end must be haunting Luke too, because at break-fast the morning after the Coke bottle incident he says he dreamed of his father. Dana is busy screaming into the telephone receiver at a debt collector, so I ask him what it was about.

"The same as always," he says.

The truth is, I never wanted to be in deep water here, and when Luke hints that he dreams of his father a lot, I'm sorry I asked. I turn to Dana, who is slamming the phone against the counter, for effect, I imagine, and I sigh before surrendering to the current of our conversation.

"And?"

"And nothin'. Why should I tell you?"

"Well, you don't have to, Luke. You don't have to do anything you don't want to."

"Ha!" he says, staring into his soggy Special K. He lets the spoon slide from his fingers and it clanks against the side of the glass bowl. "I wish I were with my dad," he says, and the telephone receiver clatters to the floor.

"Luke, honey." Dana drops to her knees beside his chair, her slender hands clutching his tiny ones in hers. "You don't mean that."

"Yes, I do," he spits, and then pushes past her and out of the room.

Dana folds down on her haunches in tears and I don't understand it: How can a woman who smashes telephones against counters and who stares angry customers into submission get broken up over what any shrink will tell you kids say every day?

"Hey," I say, ready to enlist Dr. Spock if I need to, "kids say that stuff all the time, that they want to be with the other parent."

She twists her head to stare at me, her eyes red rimmed and her nose trickling snot, and I think about how ugly crying makes her, how I feel repulsed at a time when I should feel most sympathetic. She swipes the back of her hand across her nose, trailing a thick mass of gel across her cheek, and says, "He knows his father's dead."

That's why I say Luke's personality was set when I met him: he's a kid whose mother tells him too much. The war in Iraq, mad cow disease, the tsunami, teens missing in Aruba, sharks snapping up swimmers like snacks in the ocean. And now this. I look at her, and I don't try to hide the accusatory glare, though I simultaneously tell myself to pull back, to let her handle her kid the way she sees fit, to steer clear of anything resembling responsibility.

"I *had* to tell him."

"Huh."

"He wanted to know."

I have no kids, and unlike most people in my business I don't pretend to be an authority on things I don't know about, but this doesn't sound right. "So why didn't you make up a story?" I say. "Tell him his father's a matador, tell him he's on a long-term biosphere mission, tell him he's Russell Crowe, for chrissakes."

She pulls herself onto the chair and stares at me. "Why don't *you* make up a story," she says, "and then sell it to Ron Howard or George Lucas instead of tryin' to sell it to me?"

Dana doesn't make the connection between Luke's sleepwalking, his nightmares, his fear of water, maybe even his death drive, and the information she freely offers. The kid stumbles around here like a blind drunk at all hours, and Dana tucks him back into bed with more headlines: they've arrested the child molester who lived down the block, the explosion at the water processing plant was a faulty turbine and not terrorists. *Go to sleep; all is well.*

The next day Stu calls to say he's got a line on an adaptation of T. C. Boyle's latest novel about some cult out west and I all but drool over the duct tape on the receiver. I ask him if there was any fallout over the murder-mystery-sans-murder script, the kid who promised that Stu and I were through, and he just laughs.

"Which one was that?"

"You're killing me, Stu," I say. "I need something real."

"I told you before, Bobby, business is tight. It'll open up again—it always does—but right now it's tight. This Boyle thing's got legs. Remember that stuff you did on *The Asylum?* That's what they're after, that schizophrenic rant. You're just the guy. I'm gonna get this one for us, bubby. Call you later."

Luke's staring at me as I talk on the phone, opening one eye while closing the other, like a railroad crossing signal. When I hang up and ask what he's doing, he says, "Mom says you're gonna die young."

"Well, if I keep eating her cooking," I laugh.

"She doesn't cook."

"Exactly."

"Luke," I say, sitting on the floor across from him, "what do you think I should write a story about?"

"I dunno. What about SpongeBob? Write a story about him."

"Been done. I mean a story no one has written before."

He squints and scrunches his nose and shakes his head. "They've all been written," he says. "I don't think there are any left."

"No," I say louder than I expected, startling us both. "No, Luke, there are lots of stories left, and it's bad to think that there aren't."

"What about a story with aliens? People like those. Mom says people like them because they think aliens are real, which she doesn't but she says you never know."

"Well, they'd have to be doing something they haven't already done in a movie to make it different than all the other ones."

"They could dust."

I stare at him, blank.

"Once, when Mom wasn't feeling good, I dusted and she said it must have been me because aliens sure didn't come in and do it."

"Well, I guess they could, but what else could they do?" I'm no longer mining ideas here—it was stupid of me in the first place—but I decide to just let the kid talk instead of being talked at about chaos and calamity for a change.

"They could phone home with a regular telephone instead of that thing ET had to use that caused him to almost die 'cause they had to lug it so far."

"I suppose so."

"Wait," he says, and when he shifts onto his knees I see a package of M&Ms fall from his pocket. "Maybe the aliens don't have long, creepy fingers and light-up hearts and they're not even green. Maybe they look just like us."

"That's pretty good," I say. "Hey, maybe I'm an alien."

Luke stares at me, suddenly frightened, and he snatches the bag of candy and forces it into his pocket, suddenly aware of his actual world, one of wariness and fear, no longer lost in the world of his creation.

"I'm only kidding, Luke. I'm not an alien, but maybe we can just pretend we are when we're together. Our little secret," I say, and he says, "That's just stupid." He's right, and in retrospect I'm grateful he didn't take the bait I had uncharacteristically offered.

Dana throws open the bedroom door and steps out in a T-shirt and panties, and she looks edible; I wish the kid were asleep, but he never seems to sleep anymore.

"What's stupid?" she says to Luke. "What's going on?"

"His idea," he says, pointing to me, "that we pretend we're aliens."

Dana's forehead closes in on her eyes as she stares at me, her look of disapproval exaggerated, and I tell her it's just a game.

"Well, I wish I had time to play games," she says, "but one of us has to work."

"How about we come in for lunch?" I ask. "Stu called and we've got some potential on our hands."

"Whatever."

Luke and I enter the diner at around eleven so Dana can take a break with us before the noon crowd elbows in.

"Bobby," she says before she even sits down, "you gotta do somethin'. You gotta get a gig or you gotta go."

I see now that her eyes are still red rimmed, that it wasn't the crying over Luke's pronouncement but something deeper, so I reach into my pocket and roll a few quarters across the table.

"Why don't you go play the jukebox?" I say to Luke, and he pockets the quarters and says no.

Dana sighs. "Nothing changes—the bills don't stop coming and we gotta keep eating, thank God for the diner, and Luke's insulin ain't cheap and you cost more than you make."

Well, there's no arguing with that, so I don't. "I know," I say.

"Is that it?" she says. "Is that all you got? 'I know'?"

"I've got some sticks in the pot," I say, though I feel it crawling up my chest toward my mouth, the anger, the words: *You sure didn't complain when we were eating twin lobster tails at Oliver, when we went to Paris for two weeks, when I paid for the kid's tonsillectomy.* "I've got some ideas for a script," I say. "I'm gonna buckle in."

"You mean the idea that we're all aliens? Maybe we all go around dusting the planet," she snaps. "Luke told me."

I force myself not to look at Luke so he won't think I'm mad at him, though I can see that he's bouncing the quarters in his hand, too young to know or too dismissive to care about the argument he's caused. "We were just talking. C'mon, Dana. Stu really thinks he could land this script—it's an adaptation, great writer, excited director. This could be it."

"Stu's an asshole," she says, "you said it yourself."

"People change," I say, and she stares at me before saying, "You got that right."

That rankles but I let it go. I wanted today to be different; I thought maybe we'd laugh a little at lunch, and then I'd take the kid to the Fox Hills Mall for an ice cream and then to the studio for a tour, get the creative juices going. I never get tired of seeing those gargantuan movie posters: Henry Fonda's forlorn expression in *The Grapes of Wrath,* Brando's burning anger in *On the Water-front,* Hoffman's naive genius in *Rain Man.* My Visa's maxed out but I bet I can sweet-talk one more under the radar.

We leave the diner, Luke shuffling his oversize tennis shoes over the gravel parking lot, looking himself a little like a carpet-bagger from Steinbeck's novel.

"Luke, what say we head over to MGM?" I ask.

He shrugs.

"How 'bout we stop off at the Cone Zone first?"

His face brightens a little and then he turns back toward the diner. "I better ask my mom," he says before throwing open the glass door. He comes out shaking his head. "She said no."

Sometimes I think Dana is just mean, making Luke suffer to punish me, to ruin any plan just because it's mine. What's one ice cream? What's one treat for a kid who's had to eat yogurt and kasha for the past year? Even Dana brings the kid a slice of banana cream pie now and then. "Listen," I say, "a small cone isn't going to hurt you, but you have to promise that it'll be our secret."

"Like us being aliens?" he asks and smiles wide, and I think the kid's probably not as scared as he makes out, that he's learned to navigate his mother's Chicken Little mentality and that he's got a nice little handle on manipulation tactics. I smile; there's hope for him yet.

As we drive over to the ice cream place, Luke offers up script ideas: *Two guys are playing Crazy 8s and one cheats so the other one stabs his eyes out; Mowgli comes to Hollywood to star in a Tarzan movie and breaks his neck falling from a fake tree on the set; a guy becomes a soldier to fight the terrorists and goes crazy 'cause it's so hot.*

"I want you to remember something, Luke," I say. "I want

you to promise me that when you get older, you'll watch a movie called *Apocalypse Now*. It's important; it'll change the way you think about things."

He blinks at me from the passenger side, the seat belt jammed under his neck, and says, "Like SpongeBob made me start liking spaghetti?"

"Yeah," I say, "like that."

The Cone Zone is packed, but we wait for our small vanilla cones dipped in chocolate and then eat them sitting astride a weathered picnic table. Luke looks happy for the first time since I can remember, and then he falls over like a stuntman, rigid and comical, and at first I laugh.

At the hospital I think about what I'll tell Dana; I try to corner a few doctors to ask how this could have happened, how a kid who gets three insulin shots a day could be taken out by a small ice cream cone, but they all seem to be engaged in a race, no one stopping long enough to snag. Maybe Dana misread his blood sugar level, maybe she withheld so much sugar his body couldn't take it all at once, maybe she made him so anxious about eating sweets he keeled over out of simple fear. When Dana slams through the double doors of the emergency entrance, I can't even look at her.

"What happened?" she yells into the waiting room, as if the kid who's cried himself to sleep or the elderly man with the open sores on his face or the obese woman with an ice pack plastered to her forehead can tell her.

I turn to see the train wreck that is Dana: her shoes are more scuff than white, her uniform is dotted with random stains in myriad shapes, the apron is hanging askew from her waist, her hair is steamed to her head, and her face in its anguish is an unrecognizable blur of smears and lipstick. I'm embarrassed by this thing before me, but I am also moved by a sudden realization: so this is what children can do to you.

"Dana," I say, and I pull her down into a plastic chair. She pops up as if ejected and rushes to the receptionist's window, her purse open and her arm buried elbow deep inside.

"I have his insurance card," she says, "Luke Bordman." She pulls a withered tissue from her purse, blows her nose, and continues the pursuit of her wallet. A compact, a tin of Altoids, three pens, and a roll of quarters are deposited onto the counter before she locates the card and hands it to a woman who, based on her expression, has seen everything. "I need to see him," she says, and the woman says she'll call the attending physician.

Then Dana turns to me, and I brace myself for what may turn out to be her justified anger, but instead she nearly falls into my arms, and I allow her to snuffle and smear those mascara-blackened eyes into the Armani. "Dana," I say, "I'm sorry."

She pulls back from me and stares, her grief temporarily set on pause. "What did *you* do? What happened?"

"I don't really know," I say. "He was out cold when we got here, but he was breathing just fine—I'm sure he'll be all right."

"But what *happened*?"

Here we go, I think, wondering if I should make up a story, if maybe Luke will have forgotten about the ice cream in his stupor, but of course the doctor knows everything. "We went for a small ice cream, just a small, and he didn't even finish it—"

"Huh," she says before plopping into the orange plastic chair.

"He was fine, talking about Willy Wonka, and then he was out."

A doctor who looks as if he's just walked off the set of *General Hospital* suddenly materializes before us. "Mr. and Mrs. Bordman?" he says, and my first instinct is to correct him, but I don't.

"Yes," says Dana, jumping to her feet, "where's my son? How is he? Can I see him?"

The doctor has perfected his small, dismissive laugh and says of course she can see him, but first he'd like to tell her that Luke was extremely dehydrated—it's very important for diabetics to get plenty of water, especially with this heat—and that he found something of great concern in Luke's pocket. The doctor produces a plastic bag full of jelly beans, M&Ms, supersize gumballs, and Snickers bars. "It's all right to have one sugar snack in case of emergencies," he says, "but this much sugar in a dehydrated diabetic spells trouble."

It's then that I get what I thought I had coming before. Dana spins around and slaps me across the face, then starts punching me in the chest. She's still swinging when the doctor pulls her back, and I watch the buttons spring free as she clutches the Armani with her paint-flaked claws. I didn't give him the candy, but I'll take it because she has to give it to someone and I guess I owe her. When the doctor takes her to Luke—she's leaning on him, too close, putting on the moves because that's what comes naturally to her—I notice it: the welt-faced man and the overweight woman and the sniffling child all staring at me with pity.

I walk the five miles back to my car, back to the scene of the crime, though I can't say exactly what crime was committed, and then I drive northwest until I find myself on the Pacific Coast

Highway. Ocean mist dapples the windshield as I sail past Santa Monica, Malibu, Ventura, and I take a long pull from the bottle of Jack I've got stashed under the seat for just such an evening, though I could have never predicted the chain of events that would lead to the broken seal, that first heady whiff of aniseed, and then the warm snake that moves through the deepest part of me. The road takes an unwelcome landward turn past Santa Barbara, but every native knows it's only a matter of time before the ocean rears up to claim everything, to clean the trees and the mountains and even the sky from the landscape. I drive. I don't think about anything until I see the sign for San Luis Obispo, and then I think about how empty I feel. Not hungry but not full of anything: worry for Luke, sympathy for Dana, anger at Stu, fear of never seeing my name on a 30 x 70–foot screen again. Gravel pings on the chassis when I pull off the road and get out of the car, and I decide halfway to the cliff to go back for the bottle of Jack, feeling that this is a good sign but not thinking further about why. Is it a cliché to say it's a peaceful night? Let the critics damn me to hell.

"Omar," I say as the ocean bares its white-tipped claws beneath me, "I know what takes us so long. We keep waiting for everyone to catch up to an idea that's before its time. We keep waiting for a time that won't happen until long after we're dead."

The bottle is half empty when I approach the cliff to pour some over, imagining Omar's Bentley idling beneath me. "Cheers," I shout, and I tip forward a little, but not enough. Then I sit down to think. Maybe Luke spent all the quarters I'd ever given him for the jukebox on candy, maybe he'll be in a coma the rest of his life, maybe he'll become a Major League pitcher, maybe Dana's particular brand of aggressive vulnerability will appeal to the golden doctor, who will provide insulin and Jaguars to the Bordman family happily ever after. Or maybe not. The wind picks up, and there is a tang of salt on the breeze as it brushes past me on what I imagine are more urgent matters: cooling lovers in their steaming beds, fanning flames in the stick-dry woods, caressing the shoulders of young women who pose on balconies of movie executives' mansions, their angled cheekbones and expensive breasts rising ever hopefully. *A Star Is Born,* I think, *Welcome to Hollywood, Sunset Boulevard*—this business is full of irony. Full of people who hate this business, actors who cut their teeth on broken promises and directors whose best films feature attacks on the Hollywood grist mill and its empty mantras: "We'll get back to you" and "Your project is in development."

Omar's favorite movie was *The Player;* he never tired of watching Tim Robbins as a film exec who is stalked and made miserable by a rejected screenwriter. I always sympathized with the writer: Who can blame him? Omar loved the cameo appearances by Susan Sarandon, Bruce Willis, Julia Roberts, all enlisted to walk on and say nasty things about producers. "The movie was embraced by the very people it attacked," he'd said. "That movie restored Altman to commercial and critical favor. Don't you see, Bobby? These people love seeing themselves, even when they're exposed as nasty, backbiting piranhas. They just can't get enough of themselves, Bobby. Bite the hand that feeds you!"

Maybe it's the eighty-proof alcohol or the frenzied breeze cresting the jagged outcrops, but I hear Omar say those words as clearly as I heard Dana say, "You gotta go," and Stu say, "I'm gonna get this one for us, bubby. I'll call you later." I hear Omar say, "They just can't get enough of themselves, Bobby. Bite the hand that feeds you!" Taking off the Armani is easy since most of the buttons are gone, and the wind spikes when I hold the ragged shirt over my head, surging through the arms and snapping the material against itself. When I let go, I know it will fly to the ocean, a haphazard bird craving gravity yet held aloft by a thick breeze, by a warm current, by a laughing man in an invisible car. They all march across the big screen in my brain: Omar and Stu and the kid who'd tried to stab me with a tiki torch, and then Geena Davis and John Irving, Spielberg, and the litigious director who will never again find the sky-blue arms of the Armani wrapped around his legs. And, of course, Dana and Luke, the saddest stars of the script, the real casualties of Hollywood's dark self-interest. I lie down on the rough gravel, close my eyes and see the yellow plaster walls and the egg-stained apron cinched around Dana's sharp hips and Luke's smile turn rock hard before his body follows, and then the words start moving through my mind. My cell phone rings three times before I bounce it hard across the white rocks, before I reach into my pocket for a napkin and a pen, before I write the story that will launch me back to the top.

In my dream I am playing baseball with Fidel Castro. He is at bat, and no one screams from the sidelines. His count is 3–5; when you are Fidel Castro, you get as many pitches as you want. I am playing shortstop; I am wondering what I will do when and if he hits the ball. Of course he hits the ball to me—it's my dream—and I wake before I know if I will be hauled off to prison for throwing Castro out at first.

"Celebrity dreams," my wife says. "We either dream of the rich and famous or we don't. All or nothing."

This is bunk, of course. I never had celebrity dreams before I took the medication. I hardly remembered my dreams before I took the medication. Now I dream that I am laughing with Steve Martin and singing with the Rolling Stones. I am at ease; I am in control.

"You'd tell me if you dreamed about J-Lo or Nicole Kidman, wouldn't you?" Jody asks. "Not just Keith Richards and Pelé?"

"I tell you everything," I say, and my wife stops smiling, turns to the sink or the stove, turns away from me.

If it weren't for the *Are You Aware?* quiz that our eight-year-old daughter took at school, I would not be on the medication. Her paper came home marked with red lines that, from a distance, looked like incisions, like bleeding wounds on white linen. The test consisted of ten true-or-false questions concerning handicap awareness, and most were marked wrong. When asked if disabled people want all the attention, she circled *True.* She marked *False* next to a statement claiming that we should help disabled people in any way we can and *True* next to a phrase saying, in effect, that humorous situations often arise as a result of defective wheelchairs. This was depressing, not in a staggering way—she's only eight, after all—but I felt I'd failed in some fundamental role as a parent by not being a real example of sensitivity, by not imparting in some subtle yet potent way the tenets of good citizenship. We went over the questions, one by one, and I gave names and faces to the people with guide dogs and hearing aids, wheelchairs and white canes: *Mrs. Taylor needs help reading the street sign. Should you help her? Mr. Candello's wheelchair tire is stuck in the sewer grate. Is that funny?* "But she's a stranger," Candace said of Mrs. Taylor, "and I'm not supposed to talk to strangers." At Mr. Candello she simply laughed.

That night in bed Jody edged herself closer to her stockpile of anger concerning what she calls my new approach to parenting, my new approach to life.

"Why must you take things so seriously?" she snapped.

"Because I'm a serious person," I said, though it's not something I believe but something that, thanks to her, now mocks off my tongue.

"You grilled her for an hour," she accused, slapping her novel onto the nightstand.

"I didn't *grill* her."

"She's just a kid, Lorne. Whatever happened to bedtime stories?"

"It's never too early to learn to be a good person, Jody, to be aware of the world around you."

"What happened to you, Lorne?" she said. "Where did you go?"

"I'm right here." I slapped my chest. "See me? I'm right here."

She strangled the blanket in her fingers and I knew what was coming, saw that never-ending train slamming down the track toward me. "You need to see someone, Lorne," she said. "I mean it. Ever since the accident—"

"Now teaching my daughter to thrive makes me crazy, necessitates outside intervention?"

Jody stared at me, then reached over and touched my face, and it burned. I hated when she did this, enacted her futile attempts to soften her declaration that I am too sensitive, too scared, too broken, that I need help managing my own life.

"It's not just that and you know it, Lorne. I'm telling you. Right now." Her voice chafed and scraped. "You *need* to see someone. I can't take this anymore. I *won't* take this anymore."

Dr. Michael wears blue jeans and canvas tennis shoes, and rather than the standard set of walnut-framed diplomas from Harvard or Johns Hopkins, his office bears blatant proof of his gross athleticism: tennis and lacrosse trophies, swimming medals, a plaque listing his name as captain of the rowing team. What's he trying to prove?

"Sit down, Mr. Bogan. Make yourself comfortable," he says.

Frankly, I am not comfortable in the office of a doctor who is trying very hard not to act like a doctor, particularly since he's a shrink. Have the games already begun? I sit down, he sits across from me, and I look him in the eye; I know from the start that ours will be a contentious relationship.

"You don't have any diplomas on the wall," I state.

"Is that important to you?" he asks.

"Most doctors have diplomas on the wall, that's all."

"I'm not most doctors," he says.

Arrogant bastard. "People have expectations," I say. "They're more comfortable when those expectations are met."

"Are you uncomfortable?"

I think about this for a long time, just to make him wonder. "Do *you* think I'm uncomfortable?" I ask, and he laughs, the arrogant, arrogant bastard.

He tells me he's divorced, has two children, plays lacrosse on Wednesdays. I tell him I'm here because I don't want to get divorced, that I have one child I may actually love too much, that my wife thinks I'm losing my mind.

"Why does she think that?"

"You'd have to ask her."

"I'm asking you."

Dr. Michael's office is on the twenty-third floor of the Tack Building, his windows overlooking downtown Chicago's midday clamor. My eyes are drawn to the sun that slams through, but I avert them to stop myself from experiencing the same vertigo I battled last week when I took Candace on the Ferris wheel at Montague Park, swallowing my sudden fear hard and clutching her hand harder, leaving a red scallop of prints on her stubby index finger. I glance at a steel bookcase, a tennis trophy, Dr. Michael's unnaturally large biceps.

"I'm not crazy," I say, my eyes traveling up his arm toward his. "I don't like you, I don't like this, and I'm not crazy."

"That's not what I asked," he says.

"This is enough for today," I say, surprising myself, suddenly determined to preempt his nonchalant glance at the Rolex on his wrist, his cocked head, his gentle voice an alarm clock calling time. I will see him again because I promised Jody—I will see him long enough to be prescribed medication to calm the nerves that she herself has made brittle—but I will never endure an entire session.

"All right, then," he says as we rise in tandem and I, like an angry child, like one who believes the odds are rigged against him, refuse to extend my hand first on the shake. Only later do I consider the ramifications of my act, how they betray a weak and insecure man, gift wrap the information the arrogant bastard seeks.

After my first visit with Dr. Michael, Jody is talkative, animated, already cashing in her ticket to happiness; after all, I'm seeing the doctor who saved her best friend's marriage, who talked our neighbor right out of anorexia. To Jody he is a demigod, so

I imagine she thinks that my case will be child's play, cleared up simply and inevitably, like the lightening sky after a brooding storm.

"You don't know that that's true," I'd said during her opening argument in a battle I would grow too tired to win, when she pulled Dr. Michael down from the pedestal in her mind to display him under the light of her admiration. "Maybe their marriage is still bad," I'd argued, "maybe the girl is huffing down Twinkies in the bathroom. You don't know what goes on behind closed doors, Jody."

"That's what I mean," she said. "Right there. You've grown so negative, so *suspicious*. You used to be so carefree, so happy, so . . . fun."

These indictments are why I withhold things, why I don't tell her that I left the appointment early and wandered the city, watching how others navigated the crowded streets, how they ran or slowed down to meet what life demanded of them at that moment, how much I admired them—all of us, really—for simply surviving life's sudden curves and trap doors. At that brief moment when I loved life and everyone in it, I thought of my daughter, and I ached a gut-wrenching ache that made me understand why I wanted so much for her, needed to guide her over life's rocky shoals and safely to a port in me, in Jody, in us. Was that so hard to understand? I want to tell Jody that this realization, this knowledge that we can win if we're brave enough and conscious enough and willing enough to confront our challenges, was more powerful and curative than anything Dr. Jock could have said to me. But I don't out of fear that she will later use it against me, twist it into a convenient diagnosis: mania, paranoia, whatever.

She'd find something on which to clamp down, and I wouldn't be the one to hand it over.

"So what did you and Dr. Michael talk about?" she asks, constructing a smile, a false smile, but I appreciate the effort.

"Oh, you know," I say.

"I probably shouldn't be asking," she says.

"Right," I say. "I guess not."

It is a small thing, really. Jody doesn't think so, but I am telling you this: it is a small thing. No one was killed, all is forgiven, life goes on. He was doing fifty when he hit me. All I remember is dropping my sandwich, the #12 I'd bought from Campo's Deli to take back to the office. When I came to where I'd been thrown onto the sidewalk, a quilt of faces was hovering above me. They were shouting at me, as if the collision had rendered me deaf.

"Are you all right?"

"Can you move your legs?"

"Don't move anything!"

"Can you speak?"

I lifted my hands to my eyes and stared at them. "Where's my sandwich?" I asked.

The faces flexed and contorted and winced at one another.

I continued to stare at my hands.

"Yeah, sure, man, I'm on it," yelled a disembodied voice. "I will find your sandwich."

Despite the pleas and commands not to, by the time the ambulance arrived I was sitting up, staring into the street where I noticed several people peeking under parked cars, searching, I imagined, for my lunch. One of the businessmen, sweat soaked and rumpled, came to me, knelt down, and said, "We cannot find your sandwich, but it will be all right. I will get you another one, any one you want. I will replace that bad luck sandwich."

The paramedics found little wrong with me outside of bruises, though I clearly recall several witnesses pointing at their heads and shaking them, the words *concussion, confusion, closed head injury* threading the air like sinister kites. I did not notice until I was loaded onto the stretcher that I was wearing only one shoe. What are the odds of being struck by a one-ton vehicle doing fifty and losing only a sandwich and a shoe? Witnesses say I was approaching the space between two parked cars when the green sedan swerved, launching me into a full cartwheel. When did I drop the sandwich? Whether a vision carved from reality or a purely imaginative construct, a moment has been lodged into my psyche, one I often revisit without telling Jody—excitable, alarmist Jody. It is a tactile moment, a noticeable absence when the heft was gone, when my fingers lost contact with the brittle paper bag that housed my #12 Dagwood on rye, when I intuitively *felt* I would not be eating that sandwich.

I joked with the paramedics about my missing shoe as they shined a tiny light into my eyes and asked that I keep still as they fastened the belts. At the hospital the doctor said things like *amazing, lucky, one for the books.* "The chances of this happening are a million to one," he said. I am an accountant and not an actuary, but I have to believe his numbers would stack up. So I'd used my get-out-of-jail-free card, and that is what I was thinking when Jody burst through the triage curtain, her face stained with tears, her voice a duet of anger and fear: "Oh, Lorne, don't you *ever* do that again!"

"Okay," I said. I suddenly imagined Jody on a gurney, dead, torn from our lives, Candace and I alone at the dinner table, and it was too much. "This is not likely to happen again," I assured her.

"Mr. Bogan," the doctor called before lifting the curtain. "I'm sorry to disturb you, but you have visitors. They insist." Two people trundled in under his arm, a man and a woman, both wearing cataract glasses. They had hit me, they said, they were so very sorry. On their way to the ophthalmologist, the sun's blinding glare, the flash of sudden white they thought was a rock, a child. A sudden, wrong turn.

"Isn't that what life's all about?" I asked, and I was not angry. I was smiling, and I was right. "Isn't life all about sudden, wrong turns?"

The couple looked at one another, mimicking the expressions of the people at the accident scene, and then looked to Jody, who jotted down their contact information and ushered them back through the gauze. Maybe I was a little euphoric after all the talk of beating odds and cheating death, but my attitude certainly didn't warrant the strange behavior that I began to notice in others.

When I told Jody about how I lost my sandwich, the precision of the memory, the details of the full weight of the *knowing* it was gone, she stared at me, rapt, and I see now that that innocent disclosure was a mistake. She went on about how the sandwich represented something more, a bigger loss—why else would I so fastidiously catalog it? Maybe the lost sandwich represented my first glimpse of mortality.

"Can't a sandwich just be a sandwich?" I said.

"Sure," she smiled, a smile so strained that I had to look away.

For weeks she watched me when she thought I wasn't looking, claimed I was growing too careful, accused me of smothering Candace, demanded that I see Dr. Michael. I stopped talking about the sandwich, but she persisted nonetheless, weathered my nerves and my resolve to an acquiescent finish that reflected an aging athlete in a high-rise office hawking serenity tapes and antidepressants.

Willie Nelson bows at the Grand Ole Opry, pulls me onto the stage, pushes a banjo into my competent hands. I wake up sweating and thirsty, convinced that I am to blame for these dreams because I expect them and my subconscious simply delivers them up. In the kitchen I drink a glass of ice water and stare at the wall plaque that Candace made for Jody last Mother's Day that reads, "You drove me to school, you drove me to practice, you drove me to play dates and I just drove you crazy." There are hearts and flowers and colorful blobs intermixed with the words, yet I feel a sudden clenching in my chest. I creak up the stairs and enter Candace's room. Her face is curled tight, as if concentrating on sleep, and I wonder if she *is* too serious a child.

"You do *not* drive anyone crazy," I whisper into her ear. "You are lovely and perfect."

I touch her clammy cheek with the back of my hand, and tears are drawn from my eyes as I watch my daughter in a state of unconscious perfection, as I witness a picture of unrelenting potential, as I wonder if, indeed, I might be threatening it. I feel a tug at my sleeve and turn to find Jody staring at me.

"What are you doing?" she whispers.

I wipe my eyes. I have no answer that will satisfy her.

"Come to bed," she says, and she takes my hand gently, much too gently.

Dr. Michael prescribes Paxil when the noise gets too loud, when Jody's gripes become a lit fuse, one that I will do anything to snuff. For a while I feel smooth on the medication, buffed and shiny and content. Insomnia, one of the side effects, plagues me at first, but I like wandering the house at night, the stillness, checking the window locks in Candace's room, tightening the bolts on her swing set with a flashlight lodged between my teeth. I know what Jody would think if she found me in the yard at midnight staring into the dark, a wrench clenched in my fingers, wondering what had become of that #12 Dagwood on rye. How does a thing—any thing—just disappear? Probably a stray dog nosed it out of its wrapper and the wind carried the paper off like a white flag, or maybe it was crushed under the weight of a one-ton automobile. "Why the sandwich?" Jody once asked. "Why don't you fixate on the lost shoe?" I told her I wasn't fixated on anything and she began to cry. That very night, after placing a small white pill on the back of my tongue, I had my first celebrity dream; that very night I walked on the moon with Buzz Aldrin, who put his arm around me and said, "Buddy, Buddy, Buddy . . ."

Dr. Michael asks if there's anything in particular I'd like to talk about.

"No," I say. "Not really."

"Is the Paxil working?"

"On what?" I answer, staring at the beveled edge of the football trophy on his desk that looks old but that I've never before noticed.

"Let me ask you something—"

"Let me ask *you* something," I say, my index finger cranking off a pistol shot at his head. "Would you throw Castro out at first? I mean, if you had the chance."

"I'm not sure what you mean."

"Remember, he's the dictator, and you're just some yahoo from a foreign country. He's at bat. You're shortstop. He smacks it at you and heads for first in full military gear, medals clanking, laboring in the heat. It's an easy out."

Dr. Michael stares at me.

"It's simple," I say. "Do you take control of your destiny or let your destiny take control of you?"

"Well, that depends."

"No," I say, "it doesn't. Do you act or not?"

"Maybe you do and maybe you don't. It depends on the situation."

"That's no way to live."

"That's the most sensible way to live, to make decisions."

"So what would you do, given *that* decision?"

"This isn't about me—"

"Please."

Dr. Michael looks at me, sinks a little into his chair, lowers his eyelids and folds into himself, as if he's trying to make himself smaller, less intimidating. All because I said *please,* because he now senses a crack in my veneer that he will do anything to widen. Who knew the world was this easy to control?

"Well," he laughs, "baseball wasn't my sport. It's entirely possible I would have overthrown first, even hit Castro with the ball. What then?"

This is interesting, this self-denigration, this uncharacteristic humility, the sports hero brought to his knees under the weight of the word *please*.

"I would act," I say, "and one act would lead to the next, and each act would be an assertion, would mean that I am in control of my life, that I am *responsible*. Me. It's all on me."

"Is it? What about your wife—"

The way he stops, the way he looks at me, I just know.

"What has she told you?"

"Nothing. She just . . . I explained to her that I couldn't discuss our visits, and she understands. She wants to help, and I think you should let her. Don't shut her out, that's all I'm saying."

At that moment I'm angry with Jody, angrier than I've ever been, and I imagine slapping her, punching her, though at the same time I know this is something I will never do. Who does she think she is, first threatening me into therapy and then trying to manipulate the results? Her tactics are devious, maddening, but, I suddenly realize, they are also liberating. What she's done nullifies our agreement, relieves me of my burdensome obligation. Rationales, excuses race through my mind—I've never believed in therapy, the client-doctor relationship has been compromised—until I decide that I don't need them, that I will simply allow one act to make way for the next. My eyes span the metropolitan office, landing briefly on a steel miniature of the Eiffel Tower, a soccer ball in the corner that looks too perfectly placed, and I feel *right* when I lift myself from the cowhide chair and extend my hand. "Good luck, Dr. Michael."

He stares at the shiny watch on his wrist. "But we've only just begun," he smiles, feigning control, though I see the taut skin around his lips and eyes, his body reflexively moving into my path toward the door. "Let's talk about Castro."

When I leave I feel free, confident, emboldened and wiped clean by my anger. I feel strong, solid in a way that Dr. Michael and Jody may have hoped or simply never suspected I could be, and by the time I arrive home I am laughing the laugh of the validated, the vindicated, the victor. Jody and Candace look up from a sea of crumpled construction paper.

"What's so funny, Daddy?" Candace yells as she jumps into my arms. "What's so funny?"

I look at Jody, the worry lines etched into her pretty face, and my anger is not so much diminished as tempered. I lay Candace into the colorful ocean and slosh through it myself, splashing Jody with paper, fake swimming around the living room floor. Jody smiles tentatively, and in a flash I consider saying *sandwich,* relishing the newfound control I wield with just one word, but I understand that there is a monumental difference between anger and cruelty.

"What's so funny, Daddy?" Candace yells as she kicks paper into the air.

"You are," I say, and she squeals as I tickle her arms and legs.

We go to Seafood Bay for dinner; we talk like pirates and crack crab legs with our hands. We laugh. To other diners I imagine we look happy, normal, well adjusted, though I would argue that there is no such thing. They don't notice the crease in my wife's forehead as she watches me, the bulge from the bottle of pills in my pocket. They don't know that later I will make a final midnight pilgrimage to the backyard, that I will carry a red, rubber-handled shovel in my left hand, that I will think of Dr. Michael, not unkindly, as I dig a deep, deep hole where I will bury my anger alongside the small plastic bottle of pills.

"Goodbye, Buzz," I will say. "Goodbye, Mick, Willie, Pelé." I will stamp on the moist earth before sliding the grass on top, and I will envision Castro running under the sun, arms pumping, an image of marvelous determination. At that moment he is focused on his own life, this one act that will lead to the next and the next, an image of faith in self-preservation through pure will.

I'll look up to see my wife staring at me from our bedroom window, and I will be spiked with the sudden insight that watching me is her act of survival, her attempt to take control of her own life. *Come downstairs,* I'll want to shout, *and dig a hole.* But she has yet to learn that she has something to bury, that my experience was a trigger for her own anxiety, that the fear she sees in me is her own, unleashed by a freak accident, a lost shoe, a sandwich sailing into the void.